First Degree Murder

M. J. Weatherall

First published in 2022 by Blossom Spring Publishing
First Degree Murder Copyright © 2022 M. J. Weatherall
ISBN 978-1-7391561-9-0
E: admin@blossomspringpublishing.com
W: www.blossomspringpublishing.com

Acknowledgements

For my friends: Harrison, Sammy, Louise, Beth, and Morgan – who *know*.

For my family: my mother – who was my inspiration for murder; my father – who has been proud of me from the very first; and my siblings for driving me to move away for university and thusly giving me the material I needed to write this...

I would also like to give special thanks to my publisher, to my Twitter *fam*, and my readers for choosing me time and time again.

Ambleside

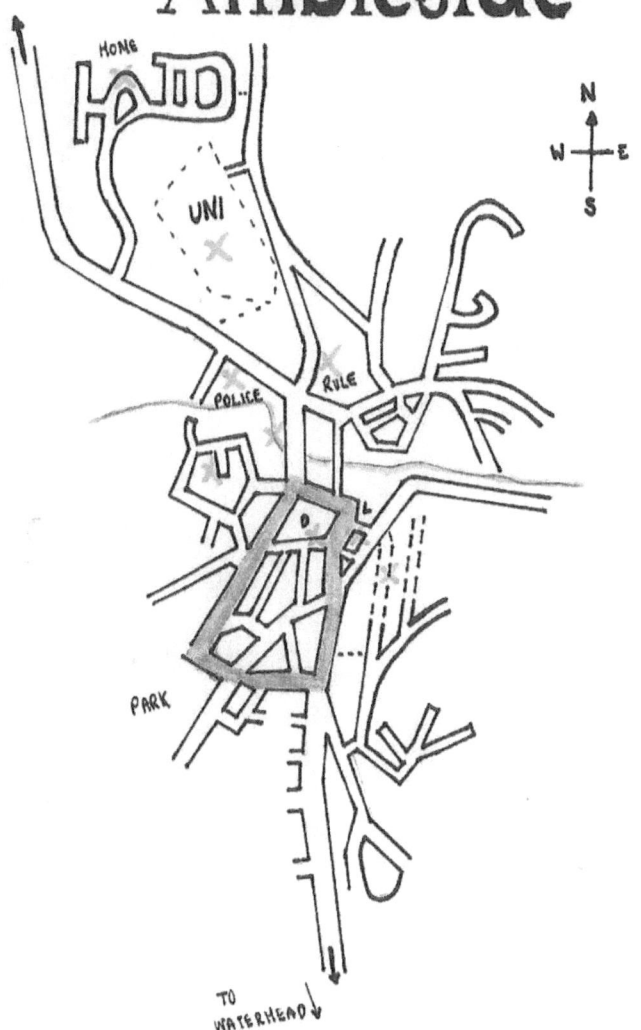

2nd June 2020

Dear Diary,

Diaries are meant to be private things. Something that no-one else is ever supposed to read. A place to dump all the emotions and events that are too hard to deal with at the time. That's what I use my diary for. All my secrets. All my emotions and fears are poured into these messy pages.

But the thing about diaries is that they always end up in the hands of people who aren't meant to read them. No matter how hard you try to keep them safe.

My name is Matilda Darcy, and this is the story of... well, you'll see.

PART ONE

SARAH

3rd January 2020

Dear Diary,

Christmas is over. It was nice spending time with my family, but I'm glad to get back to University. Even though my friends and I talked often and did Secret Santa, I missed them. I always love trying to figure out who has who each year, this year was no different. I figured out that Hugh had me and wasn't surprised when he got me the PS4 game I'd been going on about, *Between Two Worlds*. I had Jamie, which was easy, I got him a cute brass compass since he'd broken his on a mountain a few weeks previously. All in all, it was pretty good, each person showing how much they knew the other by their choice of gift.

My New Year's resolution, I've decided, is to get more experience in my field. I want to see if the police could let me shadow a criminal profiler or an offender case administrator. But I'm going to have to ask my auntie, since the constabulary in Ambleside is tiny, and she's Chief Superintendent of Manchester Metropolitan Police. Another resolution is to journal more; I keep falling behind on writing and want to stay on top of it.

Today, I am driving back up north. I'm supposed to be packing but thought I'd start on one of my resolutions while I had my diary in my hand!

I'm not looking forward to seeing Dean again. He broke my heart, not to sound dramatic, but it's true.

We study different courses, so I probably won't run into him on campus. I don't plan on drunk texting him either, but that's a whole other thing...

I started keeping a diary when I was twelve. It was somewhere for me to explore my emotions and vent about what I was feeling, without actually telling someone what I was feeling. Sounds strange, I know, I retired my first diary when I went to University. I decided I would start fresh, keep some of the sentimentality out of it and stick to the facts. Because I'm a grown-up now and don't have time to sound like a mushy teenager, right?

This mentality didn't last for long. Sticking to the facts was hard when you're writing about your own life. Of course you have to be emotional! That's a part of being alive! I remember my first entry when I moved into Halls and my family had left. I tried so hard to remain calm and collected, excited about my new life, When, in actual fact, I was alone. I'd moved hours away from all my friends and family. I didn't know anyone, I didn't know how to live on my own. I grew up sharing a room with my sister so I had never actually been alone. Ever.

It all came out. I released everything into these pages, everything I tried so hard to keep bottled up.

The thing about living with girls is the toxicity. Not all girls, but it didn't have to be *all* girls. They pretend to be your closest friends, but then when stuff gets difficult they turn on you. Out you and

4

spill all your secrets. And for what? Some other toxic girls to like them? To be the centre of attention?

It's hard to understand the motives of sociopaths.

Some people never learn, and I hate to say that I am one of those people. Call me an optimist. Or just plain naïve.

* * *

It was the day I returned to Uni after the Christmas break, rolling my suitcase from my car to our student house. Some of the people I lived with were hell on earth. It was hard to imagine that some people could be so disgusting and ugly in their personalities. But I managed to find them.

On the other hand, I'm living with some of my best friends. The guys are actual dreamboats, the greatest friends I could wish for, and their girlfriends are my best friends, and they're here so often it's practically like they do live here. It's such a shame that my time with them has to be so tainted. It's not that I'm a bad judge of character. I may have had a lapse in judgement, but it's common knowledge that sociopaths charm and seduce people to create a rose-tinted version of themselves. Anyway, I'm getting ahead of myself.

There wasn't much snow left on the ground. The warm winter sun had melted the icy formations until they were thinly spread, only appearing in the shadowy crevices of the footpaths and the smallest alleys between buildings. It made rolling my suitcase annoying, but it didn't stop my progress.

Our house is large for a student house. It was once a children's home, but now it's owned by some stingy landlord wanting to swindle students out of their maintenance loan. The building had been poorly converted with four extra bedrooms and two extra bathrooms crammed onto the ground floor to maximise their profits. This meant that there are ten of us living here, sharing one regular sized fridge and three parking spaces. Luckily, I'm one of the only ones with a car, and a job that allows me to escape. It's not everyone that makes it toxically inhospitable sometimes, but I'm glad to have an excuse to leave for significant periods of time.

As usual, when I arrived the doors inside the house were all open, rendering the Seaton Security alarm system that the landlord installed useless. Several different genres of music were blaring out, mixing inharmoniously in the narrow corridor.

"Hello!" I called to no-one in particular, not waiting for a reply.

I rolled my case past the first two bedrooms and took a left before the stairs. The first thing I noticed was that my door wasn't locked as I attempted to use my key. The second was the acrid smell of disinfectant coming from all around me.

I swore under my breath.

Why, when the landlord does inspections and cleans, do they leave all the doors unlocked? They unlocked it to get inside, how hard is it to lock the door again on your way out?

Grumbling, I flung my case into my room and gave it a once over inspection to make sure that everything was pretty much in the same place I'd left it. Happy with the lack of disruption, I went to the kitchen to make a well-deserved cup of tea. I was desperate for one after driving for three hours.

I took a left out of my room and glanced to my right,

coming face to face with the bizarre diamond shaped window. The window was inside the wall and allowed you to see directly into the kitchen from the corridor. I saw that several of my housemates were already milling around in there. I continued on, excitedly thrusting open the fire door with more gusto than necessary.

"Hey," I announced as I rounded the corner of the breakfast bar.

Thankfully, there was ample cupboard space for the ten of us in the kitchen. Although, there was still an abhorrent lack of cutlery.

"Matty, hey!" replied Hugh, a large smile on his face as he rose from one of the stools to envelop me in a welcoming hug. I smiled at the mention of my nickname, given to me by Hugh on our first ever meeting. "Good Christmas?" he asked, once he'd let me go.

"Yeah, the usual, you know. Good to have a break from this place," I said, looking around the grimy, cobwebby student kitchen. "Yours?"

"Marvellous, got to see the family, which was great," he replied.

Hugh returned to his perch and looked at the others, who were excitedly awaiting their turn to give me a hug. It was one of the things that I never understood until going to University. Hugging people always felt so alien to me. But I returned the intimate pressure of each of my friends gratefully.

"Is everyone back yet?" I asked sheepishly.

The five of them; Hugh, Dee, Lily, Jamie, and Danny; sat there trying not to look at each other, not wanting to be the one that had to deliver the news.

"Not yet," Jamie replied. He was always the most upfront and honest of the group, even if it was sometimes to his own detriment.

I felt myself relax, releasing an anxious breath that I didn't know I'd been holding. They knew that I didn't just mean our housemates, that I was thinking of a *certain ex.* Was I relieved? Heartbroken? It was hard to describe.

"Okay, great," I said, reaching over Hugh to retrieve my favourite mug from my cupboard, set on busying myself making tea.

Soon conversation flowed comfortably. Each of us recounted stories of our last few weeks away. Not everyone had chosen to go home for the holidays, choosing instead to stay in Ambleside for work, or just to escape the hellish lives waiting for them back home.

We made our way to the living room where we had our gaming systems rigged up with multiple screens. A burglar's wet dream.

After hours of anxiety filled zombie killing, I bade goodnight to the group and went to bed.

My room is one of the cheapest in the house. It's just large enough to hold a single bed, wardrobe, desk, chest of draws, and the standard sink that every student room had. I tried re-arranging the furniture several times since moving in, to find the holy grail of *feng shui*, but the effort of taking it all out into the corridor and drawing up the plans was too much. I'd given up, leaving it in the arrangement that allowed for the most floor space – something that made the room feel infinitely bigger. Or so I convinced myself.

I flicked on the big light and crossed to the blinds. I'd installed them because I was sick of the creepy neighbours staring in. There wasn't much room to hide out of line-of-sight. Despite not getting permission from the landlord, the blinds had remained intact. I smiled as I closed them. It wasn't much, but it felt like a victory.

I continued on with my night-time routine. I made sure

to wash my face and brush my teeth before changing into fresh PJs and sliding into the clean sheets. I always made sure to change them before I went anywhere. I loved the feeling of crawling into bed when it smelled so fresh and felt so crisp.

I was asleep as soon as my head hit the pillow.

I always had weird dreams, but that night was different. Everything felt so real and lucid; it was hard to tell whether I had actually woken up and done those things. When I awoke the next morning, I was in the same position I'd fallen asleep in. My door was still locked and nothing in my room had moved. I sighed with relief. There was a certain amount of anxiety I put away for my sleepwalking alter ego. I wasn't ready to have to deal with her in the new year.

Uni was due to start in two weeks, giving us enough time to get settled back into life away from home and make sure that our brains are well rested. Naturally, we took this opportunity to cram in all the partying we couldn't do during the semester. This year was no different.

I showered and dressed before heading to the kitchen. It wasn't unusual that I hadn't encountered anyone yet that morning. Since I was the first to bed it was probable, but not definite, that I would be the first one of us to wake.

To say I was surprised when I saw her standing there was an understatement. I accidentally let the fire door slam behind me. I winced as the noise shook my bones, realising that I could no longer escape without being rude.

"Morning," I ventured, not expecting a reply.

"Hey," Caitlyn replied after a long pause. The look on her face was that of pitiful sadness, and also somehow bursting to say more. It annoyed me more than words could say.

I made a cup of coffee in preparation for the long day ahead and sat at the breakfast bar, my phone in my free hand, ready to scroll through social media by way of avoidance. I was quite content with no further conversation attempts. I was glad when she left the kitchen shortly after.

I scrolled through my social media, not paying attention to the bulk of the posts. I was trying to find what I was looking for without searching his name. Because that would have seemed desperate.

My heart broke all over again when I saw it. He was back. Which meant... He would be at the party later. I sent a message into the group chat with my best girl friends, trying not to enter full-panic-mode.

Me: SOS – He's going to be there tonight!

Dee: No way!! Are we still going?

Lily: Of course we are still going! Screw that guy, he's missing out.

Me: Aaaaaaaaaaagh.

Lily: You got this, we won't let you do anything stupid.

Dee: Sure, unless it's super funny and then I might.

Lily: D! Not cool! I've got your back, girl.

Dee: But remember the time she called Jess out on her bull and then just danced away? That was sick.

Me: Yeah and all she did was dump our friend, this will

be so much worse, what if I ... cry?

Dee: Oh man, that is sad.

Lily: You won't cry! You'll be with us and it'll be fun!

Dee: Yeah!! What are you going to wear?

Dee: And if you say jeans and a nice top, I WILL MURDER YOU!!

Me: I don't know anymore! You have free reign of my outfit choice tonight, I can't even.

Dee: Yes!! You won't regret this!!

Dee: Well you might regret this but you are going to look so hot it won't matter!!

Me: Thanks girls, see you at 8?

Lily: I'll see you at 8, you know D is never gonna be ready by then.

Dee: Rude!! See you tonight!!

I put down my phone on the countertop and smiled. If tonight was going to be a bombshell, then at least I had my two idiots to help me through it. There was no way I could survive seeing Dean again without them. He broke my heart less than a month ago, and I most certainly was not over him. With my track record I wouldn't be over him for another two years.

I had so much to do that I couldn't sit there fantasising

about all the ways I was going to make a fool out of myself at the party. Thankfully, there was shopping to get and work schedules to organise. Life went on.

* * *

The doorbell rang at 7:51p.m. It was usually my job to go and open it, but since I knew who the ringer was, I didn't mind that much.

Lily was beaming at me with her cute, crooked smile, and her sweet doe eyes.

"Hey girl!" she shrieked, holding up a bottle of cheap white wine.

"Hey! Come on in."

I went to the kitchen to grab two mugs before coming back to see that my best friend had already made herself at home. She was laying on my bed animatedly wafting her arms about like she was making a snow angel.

"Aaaaah, your bed is so comfy, remind me why we have to go out tonight and can't just stay here and get drunk?"

"Because we already promised the guys we would go," I retorted, holding out the mugs so that she could fill them.

"But, but, but – they live here, too!"

"Lily! You are such an old lady, come on, we are going out."

"Fine."

I took a long drink from my wine and winced. It was *really* cheap wine.

In the time it took Dee to arrive we'd nearly finished the bottle. We were getting into some very deep conversations about the serial killer Ted Bundy and the series we had watched about him on Netflix. No wonder we all studied Criminal Psychology; we all loved seeing how serial killers thought and operated. From afar, of course.

She didn't ring the doorbell. Instead, she came to the window and stuck her hand through, trying to scare us. Which definitely *didn't* work.

I hopped up and let her in at 8:52p.m. – nearly an hour after Lily arrived.

We left the house at 9:30p.m. with the guys and made our way down the long road through our estate and into Ambleside. One of the perks of living where we did was that the walk to Uni only took five minutes. The downside was that it took ages to walk anywhere else in Ambleside. By ages, it was like twenty minutes max, but still.

We arrived at the party at 9:55p.m., which was considered early by many standards, even though we'd stopped by Tesco to buy more alcohol. Hugh and Jamie took the lead up the steep hill to the private student houses.

The door was wide open, and the party was spilling out onto the street. People with bottles of beer and cigarettes in hand were talking loudly, despite the music not reaching beyond the front door.

We made our way up through the house to the main kitchen, the epicentre of the party. It was a tiny kitchen situated on the second floor that had an adjoined dining/living room. People often used the window in the bathroom next door to climb out onto the fire escape to smoke, or to talk away from prying eyes.

I looked around the room, surveying the faces of peers that I hadn't seen in weeks, looking for the one face that was going to ruin my evening. But he wasn't there. I turned to Lily and Dee. They'd put down their belongings and were opening tinnies of fruity cider within minutes of arrival.

We clinked our drinks together dully and drank. The refreshing sweetness of the cider was a pleasant contrast to the wine that Lily had brought. I took another gulp.

"Slow down there!" a voice came from behind me.

My body froze. I knew that voice. It took every fibre of my being not to spit-take my drink and spin around to look at him.

"Dean," I replied, turning around slowly and inclining my head politely. "Didn't think you'd be here tonight; thought you'd given up fun."

"Nice to see you haven't changed." His eyes were glazed over like he was already either drunk or high. Or both.

Lily and Dee couldn't contain themselves. They burst into cackled laughter. Dean smiled and disappeared into the throng of people.

"That was amazing!" Dee shrieked, slapping me on the arm happily.

"C'mon, let's play beer pong," I begged Jamie, pulling on his bare arm until he caved.

"Fine, Matty and me against Hugh and Dee?" he asked the group, beaming stupidly.

"Sounds perfect to me," said Hugh, looping his arm over Dee's shoulders, making an intimidating face. "We're gonna crush you."

"Yeah, right," Lily scoffed from the corner.

Hugh turned to give her a confused glare.

"We all know Matty is the best pong player in this room."

"Out of all the girls, maybe" Hugh bragged, puffing up his chest. "If Danny was here, then it would be the end for you dweebs. No offence, babe," he added to Dee to save himself after insulting his girlfriend's pong game.

"Oh yeah? We'll see about that," I replied, choosing to

ignore the last part. A competitive glint twinkled in my eye.

Everyone in the room moved to the edges as we set up the beer pong cups along the main table. The onlookers watched with intrigue as we trash talked each other and poured the drinks.

"Ready?" I asked Jamie.

"Ready," he replied, his boyish grin filling me with confidence.

"Okay," Lily shouted above the noise of the music. "Heads or Tails?" she asked, looking at Hugh and Dee.

"Tails never fails!" Hugh blurted, banging his chest like a caged gorilla. Dee nodded her approval.

"Okay, Tails and it's Hugh and Dee to throw first. Heads and it's Jamie and Matty," Lily shouted, concentrating on the 50p coin in her hand. She took a deep breath and flipped it, caught it, and slapped it down on her other hand. She didn't uncover it for several seconds, building the tension.

The room was almost silent of chatter, everyone watching the game unfold.

"Tails!" Lily announced.

"Yeah! Huh!" Hugh grunted, accepting the ping pong ball from Lily with a curtsy.

The game didn't last very long; with Jamie and me on the same team, Hugh and Dee didn't stand a chance. We sunk each of our shots and hardly conceded. The more the opposition had to drink, the progressively worse their shots got.

The pressure was on when it came to the final throw. Dean was in my eyeline. I could feel my legs turning to jelly. It was my shot, and after talking myself up so much I was now worried that I would lose the game for us and embarrass myself in front of Dean.

I took a deep breath and rolled the ball in my hand,

trying not to think too much about it. That was the key, let muscle memory make the shot.

I sunk it.

The room erupted, cheering and chanting my name. Jamie was ecstatic. He grabbed me around the middle and lifted me into the air, screaming like a football hooligan.

I looked over Jamie's ginger mane to where Dean was standing. I saw him nodding and smiling at the crowd with a sombre expression, as they cheered my name over and over. I lost sight of him when Jamie placed me delicately on the ground, apologising for grabbing me so roughly. I shook my head, accepting his apology, grinning ear to ear.

After such a hype game, everyone wanted a go. Teams immediately formed and the table was commandeered, forcing us to take up residence elsewhere. I grabbed my cider and made for the fire escape. The excitement and the noise were getting to me and I needed some fresh air.

Once out there, I leant on the rail and looked out across the hills. It was pitch black. The moonlight made it possible to see the shapes and profiles of the surrounding mountains.

"It's beautiful, isn't it?" a voice behind me mentioned.

"Bloody hell!" I shrieked, jumping with fright.

"Didn't mean to scare you."

"Then don't sit in the dark, creep. You could have announced yourself when I climbed through the window."

"Yeah, sorry," Dean laughed. "It was funny, though."

"You reprobate."

"This is my haunt, what are you doing out here?" he said, blowing a cloud of smoke away from me.

"Fresh air," I answered, looking longingly at the cigarette in his hand.

"How rude of me," he said, putting his lit cigarette between his lips. He dug in his jacket pocket, procuring a packet of cigarettes and his trusty lighter. "Want one?"

"Thanks," I said, accepting his offer gladly and joining him on the cold, metal steps.

"You never answered my question."

"You gave up the right to my answers," I replied scornfully, taking a drag.

Dean took a sharp intake of breath, not sure how to respond.

"I'm sorry, I didn't mean that," I said in a quiet voice, focussing on the orange glow burning at the end of the cigarette in my hand.

"Yes, you did," he said flatly.

"Yes, I did, but only because you are doing that sad puppy dog thing. You dumped me. You don't get to be the sad one."

There was a brief moment of silence.

"I miss you," Dean said.

"No, I'm not doing this. It isn't fair."

"Matty, please."

"How high are you Dean?"

"That's..."

"Exactly," I said, standing up and stomping the cigarette out hastily. I clambered back through the window before he could say anything else.

Dee and Lily hounded me immediately, pulling me into the adjacent bathroom and locking the door.

"What was that?" Lily demanded. Dee stood beside her with her hands on her hips, like a good-cop, bad-cop routine.

"I went out for some fresh air, I didn't know he was there," I answered, sitting down on the toilet seat.

"What did he say?" Dee pressed.

"He... that he misses me."

"What!" the two girls exclaimed in unison, mouths

agape, smiles crawling onto their faces.

"He was high, he didn't mean it."

"Being high has nothing to do with it!" Dee squealed.

"You're high all the time!" Lily interjected.

"My point exactly," Dee replied, winking at Lily coyly.

"Guys, not helping."

"Right, you should talk to him tomorrow when you're both sober," Lily offered.

"Yeah, although I'd rather not bring it up again," I whispered.

"I hear there's a party down at Aaron's if you want to get away?"

I looked at Dee, thinking about the implications of leaving the party so soon, about what Dean would think, about whether it was the right decision. Something in me latched onto the idea and I found myself nodding. Screw what Dean thought.

"Great, Hugh wanted to go there instead anyways, I'll go grab them."

Dee slunk off and returned a matter of seconds later with Hugh and Jamie in tow.

"Pick up your tits ladies, we're going!" Dee whooped.

Lily and I exchanged glances before hurrying off to collect our belongings from the room next door.

The walk down to Aaron's was pleasant. No sign of Dean anywhere. The winter breeze was refreshingly cooling after the heat of the party.

"So, Dean giving you trouble?" Hugh asked as he ambled along beside me.

I shrugged. "Not really, the usual."

"Very vague."

"He just... confuses me."

"In what way?"

"I know he's not a nice guy, I do know that, but I just

can't help..."

"He doesn't deserve your help or your time, Matty."

"I know..."

"Then why don't you hate him?"

"I do, I hate what he did to me, but, I don't know." I felt my face flush with heat, whether it was anger or frustration at not being able to articulate my feelings, I couldn't tell. Even though it was dark, Hugh saw my face redden and stopped pressing me.

"Whatever you feel is valid, I just hate the guy for how he treated you – for how he's still treating you." Hugh paused and took a shaky breath. "I want you to know that I respect you, and I'll always have your back."

I smiled. "I like tipsy Hugh, he's such a sweetheart." I bumped his shoulder with mine and he grabbed me in a one-armed hug.

"Yeah, don't go telling everyone."

We walked the rest of the way in silence, just listening to the gentle tapping of our feet on the pavement, and the jagged breathing of the group.

The house was just off the main street, behind the rows of outdoor shops and student powered restaurants, in a maze of one-way streets and idyllic cottages. I couldn't remember which one Aaron and the others lived in, so I just followed along and let Jamie lead the way.

"I texted Aaron, telling him we were on our way, he said to just let ourselves in," Jamie called from the front of the pack.

He skipped childishly up to the front door and tried the handle. It swung open, letting music and voices wash over us. That was a good sign; I breathed deeply in relief. What a shame it would have been to have left a perfectly good party in search of one that didn't exist. I pushed the anxiety down – it didn't matter now.

We trudged into the house, stripping off coats and hats as we went; the heat of the small house was ten times that of the one we had just left.

Aaron and his housemate were chugging cans in the garden, smoking, and chatting leisurely with some girls I didn't recognise. He smiled and hugged Jamie roughly when he saw us enter.

"Glad you could make it! Make yourselves at home!"

We said our thanks and left Jamie and Hugh to catch up with Aaron as we found a place to stash our things.

"Shot roulette?" Lily suggested, grinning.

"Hell yeah!"

She led us back to the small kitchen where she'd seen the roulette table. People were pouring spirits and odd concoctions into shot glasses, preparing for the game to begin. They were rifling through cupboards as if they were their own.

There were several people milling around that I hadn't seen before. I recognised some from the years below and from other courses at Uni, and some I guessed had to be locals that were friendly with the hosts. It wasn't possible for everyone to take part in the game, surely? I smiled politely at the gathered people and took a seat at the table with Lily and Dee.

I looked at Lily as if to say, *are you sure this is okay?* She nodded and smiled, cupping her hand on my elbow comfortingly. I finished my cider with two long swigs. I crumpled it and threw it in the recycling without leaving my chair. No-one was paying attention to my shot because they were all looking at the newest member of our game circle.

"Dean. You better not be stalking me," I teased, trying to keep the tone light.

"Hey! I live here, remember? You're the one stalking

me."

"You don't live here."

"No, but I used to."

"That doesn't count."

"Stop arguing," a strange looking guy with a calm voice demanded. He was pouring drinks with a girl in my year whose name I couldn't for the life of me remember. "This is a safe space, no drama here, my dudes."

"Got it," I replied, breaking eye contact with the calm guy. He reminded me of the yak that ran the naturist centre in Zootropolis. Except blond. And human.

I avoided making eye contact with Dean. Knowing he would have a smug smirk on his face would make me want to retaliate further. So, I studied the others instead.

The girl whose name I couldn't remember was still pouring the drinks, doing a little bop and shimmy in time with the music. She was about average height with dark hair and kind eyes — the type of person who looked approachable, someone who would lend you their notes if you missed a lecture.

Two other girls were in the corner, clutching plastic cups like they didn't go to a University rife with eco-warriors. I scoffed to myself as my eyes slid over them. Their faces were moulded into that *Mean Girls* sneer that immediately sent up red flags for me in terms of potential friends. There was nothing I hated more than mean girls.

In total there were eleven of us playing: Dee, Lily and I, Dean, Yax, What's-Her-Face, the *Mean Girls*, and three guys I knew from the climbing wall; Tommy, Jake, and Sol. They had to be the reason the *Mean Girls* were sticking around. Some of the climber dudes were seriously fit.

"Where are the guys?" Dee asked suddenly, like they were an accessory that she suddenly realised she'd lost.

"Outside still, I guess," Lily replied dismissively, cradling her drink.

"Yeah, they'll be fine, don't worry," I added.

"Right, we are ready!" Yax announced, What's-Her-Face beaming beside him as he loaded the game onto the table. He encouraged the remaining players to take their seats. "We will go left of the pourers," he added, looking at me with an intense directness.

"Okay, yeah, sure," I blabbed, wary of being the first to spin. "Err, what have we got here?"

"Why? Are you allergic to anything?"

"No, I wanna know what I might be getting."

"That's all part of the fun, baby!"

I decided to ignore him and turned my attention instead to the board in front of me. Some of the liquids were clear, some brownish like whiskey, some of varying colour vibrancies, one that looked just like mustard, a Bailey's kind of textured one... my point was, there were no two that looked exactly the same.

"I thought the point of this was that some of them were safe, like water?" Jake asked.

"Yeah, some of them are safe," giggled Yax, What's-Her-Face joining in like it was some inside joke.

The roulette arm stopped spinning and the ball settled in front of a clear liquid. I prayed it wasn't vodka. I lifted the shot glass to my face, hoping to get a sniff of it before it went down the hatch. I couldn't smell anything. Did that mean it was water?

It was not water.

I slammed the glass back onto the table noisily as the burning liquid tore down my throat.

"What was that?"

"Guess it wasn't *agua*?" Lily chided, covering the lower part of her face with both hands to keep the laughter at bay.

"No, it was not bloody *agua*!" I snapped, seeing their faces so ready to burst with laughter made me smile despite myself. "You're next, loser," I aimed at Lily.

"I was born for this."

She stood up and spun the roulette, rubbing her hands together like she was in Vegas and about to win the jackpot.

"Looks interesting," she said when the ball stopped. She picked up the glass of brown liquid, which could have been anything from tea to rum, and slammed it back expertly. It was a marvel to watch as her face contorted. After a second, we knew that she didn't get off easy.

"Was that a bit of ol' Cap?" she asked, patting her chest nonchalantly as if it would help relieve the burning sensation.

"Yup, Captain Morgan's Spiced. You know your spirits," What's-Her-Face beamed. It wasn't something to be proud of, but hey, we were students.

"Sweet Dee, you're up." Lily patted our friend on the back roughly before plummeting back into her seat.

Dee didn't bat an eyelid; she spun, waited, and slammed the shot without much commentary.

"Was that milkshake?" she asked, her brows knitted in confusion.

"Ding, ding, ding!" Yax sang, clearly enjoying being one of the taskmasters.

"Why?" Dee asked quietly, taking her seat.

Next up was my climbing buddies, in succession, they took their shots and tried not to make a big deal of it. They had soy sauce, Apple Sourz, and banana liquor. I can safely say that the non-alcoholic one was the short straw this time. That stuff needed to be hid in dishes, not be consumed in copious amounts on its own.

It was the *Mean Girls* up next. The first one spun the wheel and watched it land on another clear liquid. Her friend with the fox face and bony shoulders leant close to the climber dudes and whispered badly.

"Sarah's really good at taking shots. She's basically got no gag reflex," which made them go pink in a not sure if disturbed or turned-on way.

Sarah braced herself. I looked at her properly, then, as if for the first time. Her make-up was immaculate. Her blonde curly hair bounced on her shoulders; her sapphire eyes were shining. She was ready to impress, and not at all embarrassed by the comment her friend made. Yes, she looked like a mean girl, but was only one by association. She was naturally beautiful and always seemed kind.

Anyway, Sarah did take the shot like a pro. Next it was Mean Girl Two's turn. It's funny, because no-one looks attractive taking a shot, that's a fact. Especially when you have to run out the room and throw up because of the shot. That's so much worse. Mean Girl Two was not as proficient as Mean Girl One at taking shots. Maybe it was her gag reflex. Her face contorted and scrunched unattractively as the burning liquid slid down her throat. Her hand clamped immediately over her mouth and her eyes filled with dread.

The game continued! Minus one mean girl. Dean tried not to cry as he forced the mustard shot down. Unlike Mean Girl Two, he managed to keep it down and chased it with some beer for good measure. He was renowned for being good with spicy food, so none of us were too worried he'd feel sick. The worst-case scenario would be that he'd have an upset stomach in a few hours when it passed through him.

"Sarah, are you okay?" asked Tommy.

Sarah had turned white as a ghost and looked like she

was going to throw up, her chest heaved threateningly. She doubled over and looked like her stomach was in immense pain. She didn't respond to our initial questions, the pain taking over her senses.

"Get her to the bathroom!" I yelled. I raced around the table to grab one of her arms. No-one else responded, not seeing the urgency of the situation. I hauled her arm over me and half carried, half dragged her to the bathroom. Mean Girl Two was still passed out with her head in the toilet.

"Jesus bloody Christ!" I shouted. I sat Sarah up facing the toilet in case she spewed and grabbed her friend.

Dean came skidding through the doorway, snapping into action. I passed Mean Girl Two over to him and, together with Yax, they made sure she had a glass of water and some bread. A classic student hack for sobering up.

Meanwhile, Lily and Dee came to the bathroom with me and were watching as I tried to encourage Sarah to throw up.

"Something's not right," I whispered, a feeling of dread growing in the pit of my stomach. Her skin was paler than normal, cold, and clammy. Beads of sweat glistened on her forehead, smudging her once perfect make-up.

"I'll get some stuff to help," Dee said, crawling out of the bathroom quickly.

I rubbed the girl's back and bent her head over the toilet bowl. "C'mon, Sarah, I need you to be sick."

"What if someone spiked her?" Lily whispered in a small, worried voice.

"She just drank too much," I replied, not giving it another thought. "Still, it might be worth giving the paramedics a call, can you handle that?"

"On it," Lily announced, phone in hand as she hurried down the corridor for a better signal.

"Sarah, can you hear me? Say something, please?" I urged in soft tones.

I was starting to worry now. If I wasn't able to convince her to be sick, I was going to have to make her. I hated vomit, but duty called. I tied her hair back with the spare bobble I kept on my wrist for emergencies. It didn't take long to wrestle her thick blonde mass out of the way.

I grabbed a toothbrush from the side of the sink, aware that if I stuck my own fingers down her throat that she might bite them off. I carefully inserted the toothbrush into her mouth. I was always disturbed by that fact, – you know, if you don't think about it you can bite through a human finger as easily as a raw carrot. That terrified me. It was only your self-preservation instinct that stopped you from doing it.

Aware that Sarah had no gag reflex, I prodded the back of her throat with the toothbrush, knowing that it might not be enough to make her vomit. I made sure to take a mental note to throw it away afterwards because I'm sure the owner wouldn't like what I was doing to it.

"Come on!" I cried desperately. It wasn't working.

"What can I do?" Dean asked from the doorway, his hands stuffed nervously in his washed-out jeans.

"I don't know, I don't know what to do," I cried. I looked up at my ex-boyfriend as I sat on the floor of a student house bathroom trying to make a girl suffering a suspected alcohol overdose throw up, tears streaming down my face.

"It's okay, it's going to be okay," he whispered, sliding down beside me and cradling my head to his chest.

Lily returned from the corridor, her phone still glued to her hand. I looked up at her expectantly. Her face was serious, making her so much more scary than usual.

"They're on the way, still on the phone if you want to

talk to them?"

"Yeah," I sniffed. I gave the update on Sarah as factual as I could to keep the tears at bay.

Sarah was still clammy, unresponsive, and we couldn't coerce her into throwing up. Her body was no longer trying to expel whatever it was that was making her so ill. She lay there stiff as a board. The paramedic on the phone tried to convince me that I'd done all the right things. That I needed to keep her comfortable and upright until they got there. The operator told us she'd stay on the phone in case we needed any advice.

Someone wrapped a blanket around Sarah's shoulders. I dabbed her head with a damp cloth and tried to make her sip some lukewarm peppermint tea, to no avail.

They sent an ambulance immediately. It felt like it took hours to arrive but in actual fact, it was quite quick. Sometimes, because of the remoteness of the area, it could take up to three hours for an ambulance to get there, caused by the lack of funds for the NHS and a shortage of ambulances. I'd learned this the previous summer when I burst a muscle in my leg, proving my theory that running *was* bad for you.

The paramedics immediately began hooking Sarah up to different tubes and monitors. Mean Girl Two rode in the ambulance with her. She thanked us for being there for Sarah when she wasn't, and I gave her my phone number so she could keep us updated.

I was glad that Mean Girl Two, who I now know as Katie, had sobered up significantly since we last saw her. Possibly because of the imminent danger her friend was in, or the fact that she'd spewed her guts up.

I'd like to say that the party pretty much ended then. But, despite the ambulance's presence, people kept on partying, unaware of what was happening downstairs. The nine remaining shot roulette players returned to the table in an exhausted slump. Not saying anything, but all glad for the company.

Hugh and Jamie came back in after a while to collect their drunk girlfriends and walk them home. Dee filled them in quickly and carefully to avoid more upset and questioning.

"You coming?" Hugh asked me, one arm around sleepy Dee's waist, the other carrying her bag like a true gentleman.

"Nah, I'll see you at the house."

He looked between Dean and me, raising his eyebrows as if to say, "Are you sure?"

I nodded. I couldn't bear to go back to the house now, so soon — I was still reeling with adrenaline.

"See you at the house," he echoed, nodding goodbye to the guys around the table.

"Don't do anything I wouldn't do," Lily shrieked over her shoulder as Jamie tried to keep her walking in a straight line.

I shook my head and smiled. Seven remaining players.

"Wanna get high?" Dean asked, pulling a pre-rolled joint from the recesses of his jacket. He had it in a little plastic case to stop it from going stale and/or getting crumpled in transit - clever.

"Sure," Yax said.

"Screw it," I said. I didn't have anywhere else to be, so I didn't mind, and I wanted something to help take my mind off Sarah.

"I have work tomorrow," Jake shrugged his excuse.

"Stop being such a pussy, Jake," Dean teased. "Nina, you down?"

Nina! That was her name. Nina looked up from her intense trance and nodded. I had the feeling she was agreeing without knowing what to. The events of the evening seemed to hit her hard. Maybe because she was the one that prepared all the drinks, or maybe she was a sensitive person. It was hard to tell.

"Yeah, we're going to bounce, see you tomorrow, Matty?" Tommy said coolly.

"I'll be there at like, five?" I replied.

"Sweet, catch you later," Tommy said, smiling.

"Later," Dean nodded in their direction.

"What was that?" asked Yax, between drags of the joint, eyeing the doorway suspiciously.

"They're Matty's climbing groupies," Dean commented bitterly.

"They are not my climbing groupies, Dean's jealous that I can climb better than him."

"I only climbed so that I could look at your ass while belaying you," Dean said crassly, looking to Yax for a high-five.

"Dude, not cool. You have to respect your lady," Yax said, shaking his head.

"I... she's not my lady," Dean said in a small voice.

Yax passed the joint to Nina who took a small absentminded drag and passed it on to me.

"Not if you treat her that way."

I tried not to laugh as I inhaled the deliciously calming drug. Dean could never take criticism well, especially when it came from other guys. It was funny as well, because it was actually kind of the reason he lost me in the first place. Even though he still never told me the reason for dumping me so suddenly.

Dean and I had been together for most of the previous year, and I thought we were happy. I was happy. He was like a love-sick puppy even before we started dating, so maybe that was just how he was with me. But I really thought we had something. When he dumped me, I was heartbroken. Before then, I couldn't have truly been in love with anyone. The pain I felt losing Dean was unlike anything I had ever experienced. It was like he was dead.

After another long drag I passed it back to Dean, who now had *the face* on, unable to make eye contact with me or the other people in the room.

Nina was quiet. Her face drawn in a constant frown, her hands clutched tightly in her lap. I watched her for a while longer before she looked up and saw my concern.

"I'm thinking about Sarah, I hope she's okay," she explained, bouncing her leg uncontrollably under the table, leading me to believe that she was more worried than she was letting on.

"She'll be alright," Yax comforted her with a soft stroke of her hair. Coming from anyone else it would have seemed creepy, but he had a weird presence that made it okay. A calming aura. Someone who made you feel worthy and safe. I wondered, then, what course he studied because I didn't remember seeing him in my lectures. I couldn't imagine the guy being a CrimPsyche student, but he was definitely very good at getting people to open-up.

"Yeah, you're probably right. I'm going to go to sleep," she informed us, standing up and stretching animatedly.

I needed to know why she was being so weird. Could it be that she was still worrying about Sarah? I was getting a completely different vibe from her than that, something that I couldn't put my finger on.

"What was in Sarah's drink?" I blurted.

"Wh- what?" Nina was taken aback at my accusatory tone.

"I didn't mean for that to be so blunt, but I just wanted to know what was in the shot that she took? Because I didn't see her drink anything else while we were down here," I said, trying to back-track so that I didn't look like a total prick.

"She can't remember what was in all the drinks. I poured half of them, and I have no idea what we used. Stuff we had about," Yax defended, waving his hand about the kitchen.

"Yeah, of course, I'm sorry," I said, aiming the last part at the wide-eyed Nina.

"Goodnight," Nina said, pushing her chair under and making for the stairs.

"G'night," Dean mumbled as she passed.

"Yep, it's time," Yax yawned and scratched his head.

"Night, dude," Dean replied.

"Night," I added, smiling apologetically.

Then it was Dean and I, alone. I looked over at him to see him already looking at me.

"Stop that," I said, somewhat stupidly.

"Stop what?" he asked, leaning towards me flirtatiously.

"I still mean what I said earlier," I added, snapping myself back to reality. I stood up and walked around the kitchen, putting the table between us.

"Fine." He offered me another drag of the joint. I accepted, leaning over the table with my hand outstretched, expecting him to tease me with it. He didn't.

"What a crazy night," I said, blowing smoke towards the open kitchen window.

"Yeah, a bit more exciting than I was expecting," Dean replied, picking up the remaining shot glasses and inspecting them. "You could have gone a bit easier on Nina, though."

"I know! I... something felt off, and I wouldn't use 'exciting' to describe it, either," I responded, biting my lip before I revealed the extent of my paranoia.

"It was just a game," Dean shrugged.

I rolled my eyes, passing the dregs of the joint back to him to finish. I looked around the kitchen again, this time opening and closing all the cupboard doors to see what Nina could have used to make the drinks. Nothing sinister jumped out at me. I stopped, noticing Dean staring at me again.

"Walk me home?" I asked.

"Of course," he replied, "but don't go expecting me to give you a romantic goodnight kiss, because you aren't my lady and you ain't getting one," he added, trying to make it seem like he was being a prick when actually he was letting me know that he wasn't going to try anything. He always had a weird way of making me feel safe like that.

"Of course," I replied, smiling back.

I ran to grab my bag and coat, thankful that they were still where I left them, untampered with; bonus. They were dry too, so no drinks had spilled on them; double bonus.

I skipped back down the corridor to see Dean standing framed in the front doorway, the moonlight bouncing off his bright blond hair, like an angel appearing before my eyes. I pushed that thought away. Dean was no angel.

"Let's go."

Dean closed the door behind us, assuming that the rest of the party goers were all inside and anyone left out on the street should be getting home.

The walk back was blissfully uneventful. We didn't speak much, apart from the occasional 'do you remember when we... here. Or, do you think that... there'. Small talk, normal things. Which was refreshing after the night that we'd had.

I never felt unsafe walking alone through our village at night. I'd done it so many times while at Uni that I'd come to enjoy the quiet streets in the moonlight. There was something about the night we'd had that made me feel uneasy. It was nice to walk with Dean.

We made it back to my house at 4:47a.m. and, as promised, Dean didn't need a goodnight kiss in return for walking me home.

"Thanks," I said earnestly as he leant on the low wall at the end of our front garden.

"Anytime," he replied, his eyes twinkling brightly in the lamplight. "I never wanted you to feel like I'm a bad guy."

"Dean, I..."

"Matty, it's okay," he interrupted, not wanting to hear the truth in what I was going to say. "Goodnight."

"Goodnight, Dean," I said, turning my key in the door silently and tiptoeing into the house, leaving Dean stood there staring up at the night sky, pretending not to wait until he saw my bedroom light flicker on and then off again as I went to sleep.

* * *

Katie (Mean Girl Two) didn't text me like she promised she would. Although, when I woke up in the morning, my phone was blowing up with messages and notifications, something that usually gave me serious morning-after anxiety.

I rolled over, drool attractively sticking my face to the pillow. I patted my bedside table until I felt the familiar rectangular shape of my phone, cursing that I'd forgotten to plug it in to charge before I went to sleep the night before.

It was 11:02a.m. and I had a lot of people to reply to.

Lily: *Anything happen with Dean last night?!?!*
Dee: *She didn't invite him in, I know that much...*

Dean: *How's the head this morning?*

Hugh: *Heard you come in last night, pleased you left Dean outside.*

Nina: *Fancy grabbing a coffee later? X*

Tommy: *Nice to see you last night! Looking forward to seeing you again later at the climbing wall.*

Mother: *R u alive? Xxx*

I huffed and put my phone down, vowing to reply to them all later once I'd slept some more and drank a gallon of water. I wondered how Nina had gotten my number. I'd never really talked to her before last night, heck, I'd even forgotten her name. I'd reply to her later and see what she wanted to talk about. I tried to ignore the anxiety gnawing at my stomach. The kind that came about whenever I needed to make an appointment or talk to someone on the phone that I don't know well. I dismissed it as classic morning-after anxiety, coupled with worry over what happened to Sarah.

* * *

It was 2:28p.m. when I woke again, to the sound of a soft knocking at my door. I dragged myself out of bed and unlocked it, opening it a fraction to see who was on the other side.

"Morning, sleeping beauty," Dee cooed, extending a mug of coffee through the gap like she was feeding a tiger at the zoo, unsure if it was in the mood to take a bite out of her.

"I love you," I replied, taking the coffee and letting the door swing open.

"I love you, too," she laughed. "Hugh told me you were out late, so I knew you'd sleep in."

"Thanks for not knocking sooner, I would have had to kill you."

"I know, we are one and the same, you and I."

She watched me drain the coffee slowly and deliberately. I felt the cogs in my brain warming and sending sparks of energy to my muscles.

"God, I needed that," I groaned, staring wistfully at the bottom of the empty mug.

"So, nothing happened with you and Dean, then?" Dee burst out. She had been waiting to ask me that since knocking on my door.

"Nothing," I confirmed.

"Boring!" Dee grumbled, checking herself out in my mirror. "Anyway, next stop – the hobbit hole!"

"What?" I asked, confused.

"We're going to Lily's today to binge New Girl and choose our assignment topics, are you okay?"

"Damn, yeah, I forgot." I rubbed my eyes and tried to bring everything back into focus. "Give me like twenty mins and I'll be good to go."

"I'ma time you, hurry," Dee threw over her shoulder as she left the room.

I lay back on my bed and groaned. It wasn't that I was hungover. It was that I hadn't had enough quality sleep. I had so much planned that I was regretting everything that I'd already agreed to.

I wasted a few more minutes staring at the ceiling before I dragged myself to the shower. I picked out some clean clothes. I decided that comfort outweighed fashion and went for baggy jeans and a retro styled sweatshirt. I ran the brush through my wet hair, fluffed it lazily, and stretched a bobble over my wrist, ready for when I inevitably got bored of having it down. Which was always.

I slipped on my Vans and stuffed my laptop, notepad, keys, and purse into my bag before meeting Dee by the door with three minutes to spare.

"I wouldn't have left without you. You didn't have to dress like a swamp hag."

"Rude. Although, I do feel like a swamp hag."

We bantered for a while longer until we reached the main road at the end of the estate. Dee didn't actually live with us, she just spent so much time with Hugh that she'd become an unofficial housemate.

We walked past the old Chapel, the Health Centre, the Student Halls, and the Police and Fire Stations before my phone started ringing.

"Hello?"

"Thank god, you're alive!"

"Of course I'm alive Mum, just because I don't text you back immediately doesn't mean I'm dead," I replied, laughing and giving Dee *the look*.

"I thought it was you, and you didn't text me back, of course I'm going to worry."

"What do you mean you thought it was me?"

"Haven't you heard the news?"

"No, what? Tell me."

"A girl died this morning. She was at some party last night and had an overdose on something. I remembered you saying you were going out, and–"

"Mum I... I'll call you later, okay?" I hung up.

"What did Mamma-Darcy say?" Dee asked, seeing the look of devastation on my face.

"She died," I dropped my phone into my bag and took a deep breath, feeling my head go fuzzy.

"Who died? Matty?" Dee held my arm firmly, bending closer to look at my face.

"Sarah," I managed to say. My heart was drumming heavily against my chest, I closed my eyes as my ears began to ring. I squeezed them shut tighter, hoping to stop the noise inside my head, hoping to drive the fuzziness away.

I felt Dee sit me down and put my head between my knees. I couldn't hear her, but I knew she was there, her hand on my back, trying to calm me down.

I hugged my knees tightly and took several long, deep breaths. I didn't want to think about Sarah. I especially didn't want to think about how her mum was probably trying to call her, the same as mine did. But she wouldn't answer, she'd never answer again. That thought ruined me, pushed me over the edge of the abyss and into the darkest recesses of my imagination. Thinking of all the things Sarah couldn't do.

I brought myself back around, out of the dark glaze. I heard several voices. Thankfully, Dee's was amongst them. I looked around to see that I was sat on the path, leant up against the low wall by the river. Surrounded by police officers in fluorescent vests and sturdy black boots. Dee was talking with them, no longer by my side. I could feel my limbs again, my brain now cleared of the fuzz, my appendages cramped and tingling with pins and needles. How long had it been?

"Dee?" I asked, my voice trembling. Whether it was from the cold or the panic attack I couldn't tell. She didn't seem to notice the shakiness of my voice, though, if she did, she didn't show it.

I saw her clearly now. Her natural blonde hair cut into a shoulder grazing bob, her hippy-esque fashion sense. Her blue eyes and familiar smile turned to me.

"Matty!" she replied, tearing herself away from the police officers that were interrogating her.

"What are they doing here?" I asked, nodding over to where the police officers stood.

"They came out to see if you were okay, I told them it was a panic attack, but they insisted on staying. They wanted to move you inside, but I told them that that wouldn't be necessary."

"Here," said the youngest of the gathered officers, extending a packet of biscuits and a weak tea in a paper cup.

"Thank you," I replied, accepting the tea and biscuits carefully, a move made more difficult by the thick woollen blanket around me. "I'm sorry, I didn't mean to cause you any trouble."

"No trouble, ma'am, don't apologise for panic attacks, I know all too well what they're like."

"Thanks," I reiterated.

"What triggered the attack? If you don't mind me asking," the kind officer asked.

"It... I... got some bad news."

"Oh, I'm sorry to hear that."

"Yeah, we just found out that a girl we know died," Dee added. I shot her a warning glance. I wasn't going to elaborate on my answer. I didn't like telling strangers things about me that they shouldn't know.

"Sarah Mooney, right?" the officer replied, now intrigued, his steely blue eyes lit up like it was Christmas morning.

"Yeah, Sarah," I replied shortly, closing myself off to further questioning.

"Did you know her well?"

"We-" Dee started but looked at me when she realised what was happening. "We knew her, everyone knows everyone at our Uni."

I drained the tea and shrugged the blanket off my shoulders before standing up. I had managed to get my breathing under control and was starting to see more clearly.

"Thank you, officer...?"

"P.C. Wilde."

"Thank you, P.C. Wilde, but we have some place to be," I said, smiling politely and handing him back the blanket and the biscuits.

"Understandable, you girls have a nice day now."

"You, too," I replied, letting Dee link her arm through mine and steer me away.

We didn't talk again until we passed the bridge house – a tiny structure situated over the river that ran through the village.

"What the hell was that about?" Dee asked belligerently, her brows furrowed with concern.

"It's the police, asking questions about a girl that died at a party we were at!"

"Doesn't mean you have to act so shady. That was insane, Matty."

"I'm sorry, Dee, I panicked, clearly."

"And you think I'm not panicking too? Jesus, Matty."

"That's not... I didn't say... mean that."

"Get your crap together," Dee added playfully, bumping me with her shoulder.

"Yes, ma'am," I responded, returning her bump.

A few more minutes of walking and we made it to Lily's without further drama or embarrassment.

We knocked and waited.

Lily came to the door bristling with annoyance.

"What time do you call this?"

"Sorry Lil, someone's been having a morning," Dee

accused.

"Ooooh, does that mean you and Dean are back together?" Lily screeched, stopping in her tracks and blocking the narrow corridor.

"No, Dean and I aren't back together, nothing happened there."

"What! No, Dee, you got my hopes up."

"You didn't even like Dean when we were dating."

"No, but I liked seeing you happy. You've been so... blah," Lily teased as she led us down the corridor into the kitchen.

I couldn't help but crack a smile. It always made me feel better when the three of us could hang out together. But, my mind kept snapping back to the party the night before. What my mother said earlier was lodged into the forefront of my brain.

"What made you so late, anyway?" she asked, as if she forgot the reason she was annoyed.

"It's Sarah. Code black," I whispered, not able to say the word 'dead', instead using a system we came up with for hiding TV show spoilers from the boys.

"Oh," Lily whispered. It wasn't what she was expecting to hear. It wasn't what any of us expected to hear that morning.

* * *

The rest of the afternoon was uneventful, we talked about our encounter with the police earlier that day and how Sarah had died in the hospital barely hours after she'd been taken away in the ambulance.

We left it to the last minute to choose the topics for our assignments and did the bare minimum of research before calling it a day. Bingeing episodes of our favourite comfort show and snacking on crisps seemed a better use of our time. It was still the holidays, after all.

It was 4:48p.m. when my phone chimed.

Tommy: *Setting off shortly, see you there?*

I really wanted to get out of it because the idea of socialising outside of my friend group that day made me want to vomit. *But,* climbing did always make me feel better.

Me: *Running late, be there at half past!*

I managed to make it back to the house, change, grab my climbing gear, and pace it to the climbing wall for just past half past. Sweating, I pushed the door open and bounded up the stairs, two at a time.

I paid at the small reception desk and shouldered open the door to the bouldering room, fumbling my purse back into my bag. I poked my head around the fake rock wall to see Tommy and Jake top roping next door. Not wanting to put them off their climbing, I sat down on the bench and slipped my Vans off.

Barefoot, I stretched carefully, making sure to work each muscle I was planning on using – which, in climbing, can be all of them, so it took me a while.

When I was ready, I slipped on my climbing shoes, grabbed my chalk bag, and tiptoed onto the bouldering mats.

The music playing over the speakers was alternative rock, which I loved for exercise because it made me feel so pumped!

I chalked my hands unsparingly and started warming up on the bouldering wall, doing easy routes.

It was a small climbing centre, created in the upper two floors above an outdoor clothing shop, but it was better than the University wall, and more convenient than larger centres in the Lakes.

The bouldering wall was a horseshoe of mixed gradient walls, each only about 10ft high, with routes ranging from beginner to expert climber.

I'd been there for about ten minutes, warming up, clearing my head, when Tommy and Jake came around the corner. Their shoes tapping comically on the laminate floor. Tommy was taller than Jake, lankier, but Jake had the classic smaller guy syndrome were he made up for it in beef. He was a seriously muscled dude.

"Hey," I wheezed, having slipped off the wall and landed ungracefully on the matting below.

"Hey! Didn't hear you come in," Tommy beamed, wiping his chalky hands on his shirt.

"I didn't want to disturb you guys."

"Never."

"You fancy joining me?" I asked, patting the chalky mat, and sending a plume of chalk dust into the air around my face. I tried not to cough or sneeze – my sneezes were never attractive. Tommy grinned.

"Sure thing, just grabbing a drink," he said, pointing to Jake and their bags.

"Sweet," I replied, grinning friendlily.

I pushed myself up and stared at the route I was attempting when I'd fallen off. It wasn't particularly hard, but that one hold took me by surprise. It wasn't as grippy as I'd anticipated.

Knowing that I wasn't likely to make the same mistake again, I positioned myself at the start tags and began to climb, shifting my weight effortlessly. I didn't realise that he was watching me until the final move when I put both hands on the last hold triumphantly.

"Sweet moves, Darcy," Tommy flirted, his head tilted slightly and his hands together, fingers interlocked.

"Thanks, creeper," I teased back, downclimbing carefully. I landed on the mat with a satisfied *whomp* and smiled proudly.

"Game of *Match*?" he suggested, stretching his hands towards the ceiling so his shirt rode up a fraction to reveal his perfect abs. I tried not to stare, honestly, but *oh my god!*

"Yes, please. Yep. Jake?" I babbled, trying to save myself by inviting Tommy's climbing partner so that I wouldn't make a fool of myself further.

"I'm down," Jake replied through bites of his apple, looking like a disgruntled horse.

Match was a climbing game that could either be really fun, or really annoying. It's basically where you had to copy the move of the person before you and add your own to the sequence. If you forgot or missed a hold, or fell off, then you were out. Playing with people of similar ability was always interesting, because then it hinged on your competitiveness pushing you to attempt moves you wouldn't normally, or, on your height – meaning you could physically reach holds that were further away.

Several rounds of *Match* later and we were all exhausted. There wasn't a definitive winner overall, but I'd definitely made an impression.

Once we'd changed back into our normal shoes and stuffed our gear away, we headed down the stairs together. It was dark now, and the streetlamps lit our small section of path eerily.

"That was great, thanks guys," I said finally, feeling the winter chill hurrying me along. I gave Jake a high five and accepted a sweaty side hug from Tommy.

"Yeah, it really was," Tommy beamed, his amber eyes lit up beautifully in the dim light.

"I'll text you," I said, before saying goodbye, looking away from Tommy.

"See ya, Matty," Jake called, looking up from his phone briefly, running a hand through his strawberry blond spikes, standing them all back on end like an electrocution victim.

We parted ways, the boys walking up the steep steps by the side of the cocktail bar on the corner as I continued on up the well-lit high street back towards our estate, all the way across Ambleside.

I dug my phone out of my bag as I walked, checking to see if I had any new messages that I could ignore.

I decided to call my Mum, knowing she'd be worrying. It made it easier to walk home hearing the judge-y voice of my mother as she berated and lectured me on staying safe at parties, and on not walking home alone at night.

I'd reached my front door by the time she'd reached her conclusion. I rifled around the bottom of my bag for my keys and hung up. I knew I was never going to hear the end of it.

I turned my key in the door and pushed it hard, parting the sea of fresh post laying on the mat. I closed the door and picked up the scattered pile of letters, about to discard them when something caught my eye. An orange flyer with the county police logo.

I dropped the rest of the post on the shelf with the Wi-Fi box and walked down the corridor, luminous orange flyer in hand.

"Matty?" a voice called from the kitchen.

"Coming!" I called, dropping my climbing bag outside my bedroom door.

I knew something was wrong with the tone of his voice.

Hugh never seemed so shaken as he did in that moment.

"Everything okay?" I asked as I pushed open the fire door and saw him standing by the fridge, Dee and Lily on stools opposite him. I looked at each of their faces carefully as I rounded the corner.

"Matilda Darcy?" a police officer in full uniform, including body cam, addressed me, reading my name off his notepad deliberately slowly. Whether this was an intimidation tactic, or just how painfully slowly he read, I couldn't be sure.

"Yeah, that's me, but people call me Matty," I replied, trying to keep the panic from rising.

"We need you to come down to the station for an interview about the party last night," he stated, scribbling something in his notebook.

"Of course, anything to help," I stammered, looking at Dee and Lily with a puzzled look on my face.

"Everyone will have separate interviews; we would like you to come down as soon as possible and not talk to each other again until the interview has concluded. We want your individual stories, not what the group *thought* happened."

"I understand, I'll come down with you now, if that's convenient?"

"That would be great, thank you for your cooperation."

"Alright."

I walked with the police officer a short way down the road without saying a word, knowing that he'd want to keep everything for the tape.

"Why are we being interviewed?" I blurted, not being able to keep my mouth shut.

"A girl has died; we wouldn't be doing our jobs if we didn't look into it."

"Right, yeah, of course."

The rest of the walk was painfully silent. I did my best to keep myself from spiralling. What if someone wanted to kill Sarah? Is that what they are trying to find out?

* * *

The police interview didn't last long. It was the grumpy police officer, whose name I didn't catch, and P.C. Wilde, the nice young officer from earlier that day who gave me tea and biscuits when I had a panic attack, sitting opposite me in the closed room, being recorded like I was a suspect. Not knowing whether or not I was a suspect. Maybe I was.

They asked me to walk them through the events of the evening. How did Sarah generally seem that night? Was she sad or upset? Did she drink too much? Take anything? Did I? They asked about my involvement – to walk them through every second of it, what I did, why I did what I did, who was there, the time frame of these events.

It felt like an interrogation. I cried, feeling like they were accusing me of not doing enough for Sarah, not trying hard enough to save her life, for having something to do with her dying in the first place. They stopped being so hard on me after that.

They asked me about Nina and Ryan (the guy I refer to in my head as Yax), about the drinks in the shot roulette game, did everyone there like Sarah, was there anyone on campus that didn't like Sarah, what was there not to like about her.

I explained everything as best as I could, trying to stay factual and keep hearsay out of it, trying not to point any fingers. I couldn't help but feel like they were trying to build a picture of Sarah being unhappy enough to overdose herself at a party where there were enough witnesses to make it an open and shut case. I didn't dare to think about someone doing this on purpose, whether it was Sarah or someone else wanting to hurt her.

When I thought they were done, they surprised me with more questions about the boys in the room. Katie, Sarah's friend (Mean Girl Two), mentioned that there were some heavy flirtations between some of the guys and girls. Could there have been some jealousy, were Dean and I amicable, am I the jealous type, is he, what about Tommy? Katie mentioned that she and Sarah had been talking to the climbers all night and had exchanged phone numbers, did that bother me?

I was annoyed with the line of questioning towards the end, but I didn't want to let it show, let them know that they struck a nerve. That would look suspicious.

"I think I've told you about everything that I can remember, can I go now?"

"Of course, Miss Darcy, this is a voluntary interview. You are free to leave anytime you wish."

"Thanks," I said, scraping my chair backwards so it screeched unpleasantly on the laminate floor as I stood up.

P.C. Wilde shut off the recording as the other officer opened the door and led me out of the police station.

We passed the waiting room and there, forced to sit several seats apart, were Dee, Lily, Nina, Ryan, Jake, Tommy, and Sol. Katie had clearly already made her statement, what with all the *mentioning* she'd been doing. But there was still someone else missing. I thanked the officer again before pushing open the door and breathing in the crisp winter air, avoiding the questioning looks of my friends.

"And here's me, thinking you were avoiding me."

"Dean!"

"Matty!"

"Aren't you supposed to be waiting inside?" I asked, giving him a disapproving glare.

"Fresh air," he explained, motioning to his lit cigarette.

"Ah," I responded, trying not to gaze longingly at the death stick in my ex-boyfriend's hand.

"Here," Dean offered me the pack, sliding one expertly out. I smiled and took it.

"Thanks, it's been a stressful day."

"You don't ever have to explain yourself to me," he replied, leaning close to light my cigarette and shield the flame from the non-existent breeze.

"Yeah, thanks," I breathed, trying not to stare at his beautifully long eyelashes as that were *so close*. I took a step back.

"Anytime." He cleared his throat and leant against the wall of the station, trying to look like the bad boy he pretended to be.

We stood out there for several minutes, not talking.

"How was your interview?"

"You know we aren't supposed to talk about it until they're all over."

"I know, how are you doing, though?"

"I... I'm fine I guess, it was just really intense, the questions they were asking made me feel..." I stopped myself, realising what he'd done. I shook my head and took a drag of my cigarette.

"I'm glad you're okay, they shouldn't make you feel like crap, you were heroic last night," he said, looking at his feet, pretending to flick the ash off his cigarette.

"Thanks, Dean," I replied, genuinely pleased and bolstered by the comment.

"Look, I should go inside now, but if you want to grab a

drink later and talk about it just let me know, okay?"

"Sounds great, I'll text you," I called to his retreating form as he grinned at me through the glass of the police station door.

I finished my cigarette alone, waiting to see if anyone else popped out of the station, but after several more minutes of waiting in the cold I decided that their interviews wouldn't be over anytime soon. I walked to Tesco and picked up some Ben & Jerry's ice cream and a bottle of cheap wine. It was definitely one of those nights.

I walked back to the house, balancing the cold tub of ice cream on my sleeve and gripping the chilled bottle of white wine with my other free hand, regretting my choice of sins on that particular winter's evening.

I spent the evening binge watching Netflix and consuming my well-earned wine and ice cream. Waiting. Waiting for a text saying they had finished. Waiting for a text to say that Sarah had killed herself. Waiting for *someone* to keep me updated.

I picked up my phone for the billionth time and clicked on Dean's contact. It would be stupid to call him right now, wouldn't it? It might interfere with the interviews. I sighed exasperatedly and threw my phone down.

At that moment, I heard the key in the door. I sprinted down the corridor like a dog whose owner had just come home. It was Dee, Lily, and Dean.

"What happened? Why are you all together?" I burst.

" *We* waited for each other," Lily retorted snappily.

"Holy crap, I'm so sorry, I should have waited longer."

"Longer?"

"Yeah, it was cold outside."

"You're an idiot," she laughed.

I let them all come inside, out of the cold, before barraging them with more questions.

"I could really use a drink," Dee interrupted, and several murmurs of agreement went up.

"Matty and I were going to *The Rule* if you fancy it?" Dean interjected.

"Ooh, yes! We can get the back room and then no-one can eavesdrop," Lily agreed, a little too readily.

I was a little taken aback at Dean's forwardness. He'd walked back here with two of my friends for plans that we hadn't yet agreed on and then invited them. The boy was confusing. He was the one that broke up with me, and yet he's chasing me like a love-sick puppy. Again.

Which left me questioning – *do* I want to get back together with Dean? I was so worried that I wouldn't be able to get over him that I hadn't stopped to think of what would happen if he wanted me back. But, then again, that in itself was stupid. Why should I consider getting back with him if he was just going to change his mind? I am a feminist, after all, why should I submit to the will of male wants and fancies when they change like the Cumbrian weather? Because he made me happy once upon a time? Yeah, well he also broke my bloody heart.

"Earth to Matty."

"Yeah?"

"*I said,* are you going out like that, or do you need us to wait while you change?" Lily asked, concern wrinkling her forehead.

"I'll go like this, unless I've spilled ice cream on me?"

"No, you're clean," she laughed, patting my arm pitifully.

I grabbed my coat, stuffed my purse in my pocket, and slipped on my Vans quickly, catching up with the three of them at the door.

"So, come on then, what did the *pigs* ask you?" I asked inquisitively, skipping down the middle of the street just in front of my friends.

It didn't take us long to reach the pub, it never did for students.

We talked for hours about the events of the last twenty-four hours, feeling like we were trapped in some 90's teen horror movie, except instead of slurping milkshakes in some American Diner we were downing pints in an old, dingy pub.

It was nice to be together like this after so much time at home for the holidays. I really missed going to the pub with my friends. Even if it was under such strange and depressing circumstances.

"Hey, have you seen this?" Lily brandished her phone to the rest of us showing a picture of Sarah Mooney and a paragraph of text that basically detailed a University wide memorial for Sarah on campus, something Katie no doubt organised. It was in three days.

"It's a bit soon, isn't it? She's not even been dead a day," Dean commented, bringing his pint up to his lips.

"Guys are so insensitive!" Lily replied, locking her phone and taking a long swig of her drink, trying not to look at the offender.

"I get were you're coming from, Dean, but you can't say things like that," Dee translated Lily's scoff tactfully.

"I heard it, sorry, ladies." Dean smiled. He always loved winding Lily up, but this time I could tell it wasn't intentional – he was genuinely embarrassed.

"They're closing up, let's get going." I drained my glass and tapped it on the sticky wooden table impatiently.

Dean had already finished his pint and Dee was drinking her last quarter painfully slow.

"We are going to the memorial though, aren't we?" Lily asked, as if we were somehow not bothered about attending.

"Of course we're going, Lil," I replied reassuringly, shooting Dean a sharp look.

Lily seemed to physically relax after that and finished her drink. She announced that she needed to pee and scampered away. She was such a tiny human that it always surprised me that she could handle alcohol so well.

We said goodbye to Reggie and the other bar staff and left through the back door.

We did the rounds of the village, dropping Lily off first, and then Dee at her place above the archway in the centre of Ambleside before heading back towards mine.

"Can I ask you a question?"

"Anything," Dean replied. "Well, not *anything*, but you know, shoot."

"You never told me why you broke up with me."

"That's not a question, Darcy."

"Fine," I replied sassily. "Why did you break up with me? You can't not tell a psychology student the reason behind something like that."

"It's better if you don't know."

"No crap, c'mon, we are friends now, right?"

"Right, but you have to promise me you won't get mad."

"I won't get mad," I promised, worried about what he was about to say.

"I did something stupid, I regret it, I didn't want to hurt you like that, so I broke up with you."

"That makes *zero* sense."

"I cheated on you, Matty," Dean spat, disgusted with himself.

"Who with?" I responded, not fooled by the show of aggression. He wanted me to lash out, to react a certain way, and I wasn't going to. This was typical Dean behaviour, wanting to make me do something that would show I was an unreasonable person, to make things easier for himself.

"It doesn't matter, it's over," he replied calmly, seeing that I wasn't going to play his game.

"How long were you seeing her for?"

"After I broke up with you, I kept seeing her, but it was just sex!"

"Oh, as long as it was *just sex.*"

"I knew you'd be like this," he said, his face not showing his delight that I was finally biting at his bait.

"Poor you," I threw back at him, intending on ending the conversation there before he told me anything else.

"You don't understand what it was like for me."

"You're right Dean, enlighten me, how was it having sexual relationships with two women?"

"That's not..."

"That's not what, Dean? Fair?"

"I was manipulated," he admitted, not meeting my eyes. I wondered whether he was being serious or if he was blowing it out of proportion to elicit some sympathy from me. I decided it wasn't worth getting wrong. He wasn't like that anyway, he never opened-up about serious stuff when we were together, so this must be the real deal.

I snapped out of the red mist at that point, suddenly realising what a cow I'd been and that I hadn't even thought of *that* possibility.

"Wait, Dean, she *manipulated* you? What did she do?" I pressed, no longer the annoyed ex but the concerned friend. My anger had been redirected to the mystery woman.

Dean told me things he never thought he'd share, things I'd never repeat; details of their conversations, their meetings, how she acted around him. It all seemed bizarre, like, who was this crazy girl? It seemed she had zero social skills or relationship experience, which isn't necessarily a bad thing, it was just odd at this point in our higher education.

"Dean, you know that's illegal? You should go to the police."

"I can't, she..." his voice was strained, distant.

It dawned on me. "She blackmailed you."

Dean nodded, not meeting my eye.

"Whatever it is, it can't be worth *this*. I'll go to the police station with you so you can file a report. Your story matters, Dean.

"So many guys dismiss their experiences because of the stigma around sex, and assaults like yours go under the radar because of bloody *toxic* masculinity, and predators like her continue to get away with it."

"I'll think about it."

"Please do, Dean. I care about you still. And I'm so sorry that this happened to you. But I want you to know that you can trust me."

"Thanks, Matty. I wish I'd told you sooner."

We'd been talking so seriously that I hadn't realised we had reached my house.

"You promise you'll think about my offer? I'll talk to my Auntie if you want and see if she has any advice. Maybe if there was a way to keep your name out of it then she wouldn't know it was you and whatever she has on you will stay secret-"

I was interrupted mid-sentence by Dean's mouth coming down hard on mine. He grabbed me around the waist and pulled me into him. My initial reaction was that of shocked annoyance, but then I relaxed into him, the familiarity of his taste awakening a longing for him that I'd long repressed. I ran my fingers up his neck, tracing the line of his jaw with my thumb as his hands gripped me tightly, stroking a line up my spine that made me shiver.

A light came on in the corridor by the front door, pulling me back into the present. I broke away from Dean sheepishly.

"And you said I wouldn't be getting a goodnight kiss," I whispered teasingly.

"Goodnight, Matty," he sang.

"Goodnight, Dean."

I put my key in the door and turned it slowly, the kiss still on my mind, I could still feel the tingling ghost of his lips on mine.

I pushed the door open and slunk inside, not looking to see if Dean was still there because I knew I wouldn't be able to stop myself from blushing.

56

PART TWO

NINA

9th January 2020

Dear Diary,

Something doesn't add up about Sarah and the party. What was in her drink? I know I study Criminology but I don't think I'm crazy for thinking something weird happened to her.

Her memorial is later this week on campus, and I'm planning on getting a better idea of what she was like there.

I can't wait for the semester to start again. I need to put all this restless energy into something worthwhile! At least I got to see what happens in a real police interview, that's a positive experience, right?

Dean and I kissed... I don't know how I feel about it, especially after what he told me about the girl he cheated on me with. Do I believe him?

Sarah's memorial took place three days later. It was an open event run by Katie and the University, which meant that anyone could be there.

Hugh, Jamie, and I went together. We were planning to meet up with Dee and Lily on campus since it was in the middle of our residences.

The memorial was held at the big tree on the hill in the centre of campus. It was a place that normally had students milling around it, reading under its voluminous branches, playing football or Frisby around its thick trunk, or sheltering briefly from the rain or the overwhelming-ness of University life and education. It was a well-loved tree; the perfect place to honour the memory of one of our own.

The memorial started at 2p.m, to give everyone enough daylight to get their grief out. Refreshments were provided in the campus cafeteria opposite. It was a lovely idea, but somehow it all felt so clinical, so forced. The vibe was weird. I couldn't quite put my finger on why. Maybe it was because of my doubts about how or why Sarah died, but...

I felt like I was being watched.

Katie was surrounded by a herd of sympathetic Mean Girls saying things like: she's in a better place now, she wouldn't have wanted you to cry, thank God for waterproof mascara.

I smiled and gave her a small wave when she saw me across the way. She nodded in return. Something I never thought I'd receive; the respect of a Mean Girl. All jokes aside, Katie did seem like a decent person, despite the stereotype I'd stamped her with before actually getting to know her. We are all a part of the problem; no-one is perfect.

The memorial consisted of people sharing their memories of Sarah and saying what a shame it was to lose her.

It was more than a shame, it was a tragedy, something that never should have happened. Something that, in modern times, shouldn't be such a regular occurrence.

I didn't want to stand up there and talk about a girl I barely knew. A girl who spent her last conscious moments listening to my terrified begging as I pleaded with her to stay with us. No; I'd said my piece for Sarah.

Katie was the first to speak.

I didn't do it intentionally, but I zoned out, looking instead at the sea of my fellow students sitting on folded seats. Their expressions were sombre and still. The occasional sad smile did a Mexican wave as Katie told charming stories about Sarah Mooney, the campus golden girl, library lurker, charity event organiser. The extra-curricular queen who could do no wrong. The girl loved by everyone for being kind, upbeat, and diabolically happy.

What does a girl like that need to take drugs for?

How does a girl like that become a tragic, teenage overdose victim?

Unless she didn't take the lethal dose willingly, or even knowingly.

Sarah Mooney had been murdered.

Of course, it was at that moment that my name was mentioned, and I snapped back into focus.

"...She did everything she could, she was quick thinking, and smart. Matty – you're my hero. Thank you."

Everyone turned to stare at me. Tears were trailing down my face, but not because of Katie's speech. No. Not *just* because of Katie's speech, but because of what I'd realised. What I was now certain of.

Speechlessly, I nodded my head towards Katie, trying desperately not to make eye contact with the masses of my awed peers, and forced a sad smile on my lips.

As the next speaker approached the front, I took the opportunity to look around the gathering. I wanted to find Dean and tell him my theory, but I couldn't see him.

I knew that Dee or Lily would dismiss my theory, reassure me that nothing untoward had happened to Sarah. That would have been the smart option, to drop it, let the police do their jobs and get on with my life. But I had a hunch, and Matilda Darcy never drops a hunch. I knew Dean would humour me, listen to my crazy ideas without judgement. He would encourage me to get to the bottom of my feelings. That's what I needed.

I slipped out of my seat and made my way to the back,

combing the sea of faces thoroughly.

Then I saw him. He had a hysterical Nina in his arms, sobbing uncontrollably, trying to say something between heaving breaths. I crossed over to where they stood by the cafeteria picnic benches, far enough away from the tree to not cause a scene.

"Dean! What's up with her?" I whispered frantically after jogging over to the pair.

"I don't know, she just started like this and won't stop, she keeps trying to say something but she's not making any sense," he replied, looking panicked, his arms around Nina like he was breaking up a bar fight.

"Okay, I'll go get her some water. Try and get her to sit down and take deep breaths," I ordered, heading inside the cafeteria at a normal pace to avoid drawing attention to myself.

The queue for the refreshments was longer than I anticipated, given that people were still talking about Sarah on the hill. I waited impatiently, trying not to tap my foot. Dean must have taken Nina around the corner to the sheltered picnic benches because they were no longer in my line of sight. That was a relief, at least.

It took nearly ten minutes to get a tiny paper cup of water. I took a deep breath and walked it carefully outside. I saw Dean sitting alone and gave him a quizzical look.

"Where's Nina?" I asked.

"She went to the bathroom to..." He looked over to the building I'd come from.

"Escape?" I accused.

"What, no, why do you have that look on your face?"

"How long has she been gone?"

"Nearly as long as you have."

"I'll go check on her." I tried not to sound annoyed. It wasn't his fault he didn't understand the female mind.

I handed Dean the cup of water in case Nina did actually come back, and quickly walked to the ladies' bathrooms. They were on the bottom floor of the library, behind the cafeteria. I'm surprised I didn't see or hear her pass me, but then again, I was facing the other way and blinded by my task.

I checked each stall by carefully pushing the doors open slowly, one by one. I took a deep breath as I got to the last one which had the red engaged symbol above the handle.

"Nina?" I called softly.

The cubicle door opened, and a girl stepped out. She was about an inch taller than me, with bleach blonde hair that fell in loose curls around her skeletal shoulders. It wasn't Nina. She was polar opposite in appearance. I apologised profusely and explained that I was looking for my friend. She smiled and nodded, but I could tell she thought I was crazy.

I sprinted out of the bathroom to go tell Dean what an idiot he was for letting her out of his sight when I ran straight into someone.

"Oh my god, I'm so sorry, I..." I apologised. I gripped his arms firmly to stop him falling over.

"No worries, in a hurry to get back out there?" P.C. Wilde asked, smiling boyishly.

He'd dressed in a black suit, his dark hair combed and slicked back like a 1920's mobster. It was strange seeing him out of uniform, and if I hadn't known he was a police officer I would have assumed he was a student at the university.

"No, actually I'm looking for a friend."

"Is everything alright, Miss Darcy?" he asked, seeing the worried look on my face.

"Yes... no, I don't think so."

"Hey, woah, tell me what's wrong."

"We have to find Nina, she was hysterical and then she disappeared."

"Nina? One of the other girls from the party?"

"Yes!"

"Alright, I'll help you find her."

"You're off duty, it's fine."

"I don't mind, but I need to pee. Here, take my number." He pulled a small black notepad from his suit pants pocket and scribbled his digits down.

"I'll keep you posted." I waved the piece of paper at him before sidestepping away restlessly.

When P.C. Wilde disappeared through the door to the men's bathroom, I ran, being more careful of who I might bump into this time. I couldn't afford more distractions.

"Dean!"

"She wasn't there?"

"Nope, where could she have gone?"

"Try her house?"

"Good shout." I patted Dean on the arm reassuringly as I put P.C. Wilde into the contacts of my phone and texted him the address. "Let's go."

Since neither Dean nor I had driven to the memorial, we had to get to Nina's on foot, so we ran. Well, jogged. Mostly. I was glad I wasn't wearing heels; I'd not mastered running in those bad boys yet.

We'd made it to the bridge house by the time P.C. Wilde cruised past us in his police car. He stopped at the lay-by and flashed us. We jumped gratefully into the back.

"I shouldn't be doing this," P.C. Wilde stated as he sped towards the student houses behind the high street, to the house we'd been partying at the night Sarah died.

"No-one should speed, Officer Wilde," Dean joked.

"I meant, helping you with this."

"You didn't have to come," I snapped, holding onto the back of the passenger side seat tightly, my fingernails digging into the leather anxiously.

"You seemed distressed. Of course I had to come."

Dean gave me a strange look like: *who is this guy?*

"I think someone spiked Sarah," I blurted.

"You, what?"

"Yeah, where's this coming from, Matts?"

"She wasn't the drug type, she wouldn't get herself into this situation," I babbled, wafting my hands anxiously.

"You even said yourself that you didn't really know her. You don't know what she was capable of," P.C. Wilde contested.

"Yes, but we all know her type. She was smart, she was kind, she was ambitious. Plus, no CrimPsyche student takes hard drugs, that's just a fact."

We pulled up to the house the party took place in, and P.C. Wilde let us out. I don't know why I was stupid enough to try the door handle of a police car, but that's something else.

We rushed up to the front door to find it locked. Surprisingly. I'd never turned up at this house and been locked out before.

"Damn," Dean burst, thumping the door hard with his fist, as if it would magically open after being abused.

"'Round the back!" I yelled, sprinting around the side of the building, using the small alley used for the bins, not caring that I was wearing a dress and, once again, glad I wasn't wearing heels.

"You can't break in!" P.C. Wilde called.

"Probable cause?" I yelled back without looking.

"Probable cause for what?" he shouted, running after me.

I thanked the gods that the window had been left on the

latch. I shimmied it open and climbed through, glad that no-one was making use of the facilities. That would be hard to explain away. Dean climbed in behind me and looked dumbfounded at my expression.

"What? I wasn't going to wait for you to open the front door," he stated.

"No, of course not."

P.C. Wilde followed begrudgingly.

We raced through the kitchen and up the stairs to the bedrooms.

"We don't know which room is hers."

"Start knocking."

I knocked urgently on the closest door.

After a second's hesitation and rustling beyond, Ryan opened it, wearing just his boxers.

"Hey, Matty! What can I do you for?" If he looked surprised to see me, he didn't show it.

"Ryan? Why aren't you at the memorial?" I asked, momentarily distracted from the reason I had knocked on his door in the first place.

"One – people grieve in different ways, my dude, and two – you knocked on my door, you can't be surprised that I answered it."

"Both exceptional points."

"Thank you," he answered, bowing his head.

"Anyway, we're looking for Nina, which room is hers?"

"Number three, why?"

"Number three!" I yelled to Dean and P.C. Wilde. "I'll explain later, thanks Ryan."

Ryan nodded slowly before closing the door, not waiting to see what I was going to do next.

"Nina! Open up. It's P.C. Wilde," he shouted, knocking forcefully on the door.

"We don't have time for this," Dean snapped. He

pushed P.C. Wilde aside and tried the door handle. "It's locked."

"She might not be in," P.C. Wilde suggested naïvely.

Dean gave him a sympathetic look before switching to full macho mode, attempting to kick the door down. He cursed and held his ankle.

"Damn it." P.C. Wilde, looked from Dean to the door. "If anyone asks, it was you," he said, right before he kicked the door open.

"Gotcha," Dean whimpered, hopping dramatically on one foot.

P.C. Wilde was the first inside. He swore loudly and closed the door in my face. I heard the deadbolt slide and my heart nearly stopped.

"Hey! What the hell?" I banged on the door with the flats of my hands.

"Matty, please. Don't come in." P.C. Wilde's voice was strained, holding back emotion.

"Wilde, what is it?" Dean called, beside me.

"I've got Nina."

With those three words I knew it was over. The horrible gut feeling I'd had leading up to this, from the moment I arrived at the memorial, to the moment Nina left my sight subsided, leaving me feeling hollow again. I looked at Dean and saw him realise it too. Nina was dead.

"No..." He looked at me as if I could change the outcome, prove him wrong. But I couldn't.

I watched him break in front of me, and it was unbearable. I caught him as he sank to his knees, before he hit the ground, sobbing angrily into my coat. He gripped me painfully tight, but I didn't mind.

I could hear P.C. Wilde's voice as he called it in. He was shaken, too. I couldn't imagine having the strength he had to stay so calm in that moment.

Within minutes, several more police vehicles arrived on the street in front of the house, lights on, sirens silent. Ryan, Aaron, and the other students were evacuated in order for the Crime Scene Investigators to do their job. Dean and I were taken to the police station along with P.C. Wilde, who was being treated the same as the two of us. His boss was angry that he went along with our hunch, so he was treating him like a reckless student, too.

It took hours for the police to get around to questioning us. I don't know if this was an interrogation tactic, or if they were waiting to hear more details from the crime scene so that they could ask more informed questions.

Another long wait in the police station was not what either of us were expecting, but there we were. P.C. Wilde wouldn't look at us, let alone talk to us. I could understand that he was worried about his job and traumatised by what he saw, so actually, yeah, I would probably be the same in his position. I left him alone.

I looked at my phone, thinking I should probably tell my friends what had happened so they wouldn't worry that they'd lost me on campus. What, with all the death going around.

I stroked Dean's thick, fair hair as he lay with his head on my lap.

"Matty?"

"Dean?"

"I'm sorry."

"You have nothing to be sorry for."

"I shouldn't have let her out of my sight."

"You weren't to know."

"You knew."

"Yeah, well... People are kind of my thing."

"Yeah, trees are my thing. I'm rubbish at people."

I continued to stroke his hair. Thinking about Nina,

thinking about how I wasn't actually that good at people. If I was smarter, then I could have saved Nina. I could have saved Sarah.

* * *

They took us all in individually and interviewed us. Taking us in again and again as they received more information between the three of us. The questions P.S. McNally asked were strangely specific, yet I couldn't get a sense of the police's angle.

"Why did you follow Miss Stanley home?" he asked.

"She was hysterical at the memorial, and I wanted to make sure that she was okay. She was trying to tell Dean something before she disappeared, but we couldn't make out what it was."

"How well did you know Miss Stanley?"

"I didn't know her that well, I saw her around campus, and we were at the party the other night, playing the same game."

"You didn't know her well, but you knew where exactly she lived?"

"Yes, from the night of the party, we were playing a game in her kitchen."

"Did Miss Stanley say anything to you at the memorial to lead you to believe she would take her own life?"

"We couldn't make out what she was saying, she was hyperventilating, that's why we were trying to find her."

"Why do you think she did it?"

"Why does anyone do anything? I don't know what you're wanting me to say here, officer."

"Alright. What was Miss Stanley like?"

"She was nice, quiet, hung around with Ryan Scott a lot, that sort of group."

"Okay, I'll look into Ryan Scott. What part did P.C. Wilde play in all this?"

"I bumped into P.C. Wilde at the memorial, he saw that I was distressed about losing Nina and he wanted to help."

"What is the nature of your relationship with P.C. Wilde?

"P.C. Wilde is a police officer, that's the only capacity I've known him in."

"Then why did he help you?"

"He was doing his job."

"Was it P.C. Wilde's idea to break into the student house?"

"No. It was my idea."

"You mentioned to P.C. Wilde that you thought Sarah Mooney had been spiked, can you elaborate on that?"

"I think she was spiked. How else would she have died so suddenly? Without warning, or showing signs of stress or depression before?"

"Mr Walker says that Miss Stanley didn't confide anything to him at the memorial. Yet, he was certain that she was going to harm herself?"

"Yes, I've told you already, Dean couldn't understand what she was saying, we followed her to make sure she was okay. He didn't think she was going to hurt herself. He didn't even know she went to the bathroom as an excuse to escape."

"Forgive me, so you were the one worried she would harm herself. Why?"

"I'm a Criminology and Psychology student, I know people. Nina was showing severe signs of stress at Sarah's memorial. Maybe I was being paranoid, but I was right, wasn't I?"

"What was Mr Walker's relationship with Miss

Stanley?"

"You should ask Dean that. As far as I'm aware they didn't really know each other. She

lives – lived – in the house he used to live in."

"Thank you for your cooperation, Miss Darcy. If we require further information, we will contact you."

I was exhausted by the time we were let go. P.S. McNally was such a hard ass.

When two girls die in the same house just days apart, it should start to look suspicious! I couldn't believe they weren't taking my worries about it seriously. Or maybe they were and weren't allowed to tell me. Maybe we were their prime suspects.

An officer escorted each of us home and informed us that we weren't suspects, but that we should try and keep a low profile for the next few days.

* * *

I tried to heed the police officers warning, but it was killing me to stay inside for so long. When the opportunity to escape arose, I took it.

Tommy: *Fancy a climb?*

Me: *YES!*

Tommy: *We'll be down at 3! x*

Me: *See you at 3! x*

I didn't know who *we* were but hopefully it was just Jake and Sol. Otherwise, my social battery probably wouldn't be able to take it. I paused before matching his kiss at the end of the second message, unsure what the consequences of it might be. I figured there was no harm in it, it might lead somewhere, or it might not.

I looked at the clock, figuring there was no harm in setting off early. I grabbed my bag, stuffed it with my climbing gear, purse, keys, water bottle, and a healthy snack.

After the stress of being stuck inside for the past two days waiting to hear back from the police, I needed to burn off some restless energy. I would not do well in prison. Not that I was going to prison. Probably.

I left the house giddily, shouting to Hugh that I was only going climbing and that I'd try to stay out of trouble. I slung my bag over my shoulder and skipped down our front path, before catching myself and forcing myself to act more normal.

Me: *How are you handling suspension?*

P.C. Wilde was dodging most of my texts, it was only a matter of time before he gave in and texted me back.

I slipped my phone back into my bag and strode down the street purposefully, keeping my eyes on the ground.

I reached the climbing wall at 2:45p.m. which gave me enough time to stretch and warm up before the boys arrived.

My phone buzzed in my bag.

P.C. Wilde: *Cautious optimism with a side of realism. How are you?*

Me: *That's fair. I'm okay, out climbing with friends* atm*, needed to burn off some stress.*

P.C. Wilde: *If you get into trouble, I am not coming to save you this time!*

Me: *Trouble? Me? How dare you, sir!*

I was smiling at my phone like an idiot when they walked in.

"Hey!" Tommy beamed, leading the group. He leant in and gave me an unexpected hug.

"Hey!" I replied, matching his enthusiasm.

"Hey, Matty, hope you don't mind that I brought a friend." Jake 'bro' punched me on the shoulder and winked.

"Not at all, the more the merrier," I replied with a confused smile.

Behind Jake came Sol who was chatting to a girl I didn't instantly recognise.

"Hey, Sol."

"Hi, Matty, have you met Skye?"

"Hi, Skye, I think we've met... once."

"In the bathroom at Sarah's memorial. Awh, I'm really sorry about what happened to your friend. It's nice to be properly introduced."

"Yeah, thanks."

They strode past me in single file to pay at the desk. I couldn't help but feel that it was a strange social interaction. But then again, it could be that I hadn't left the house in two days and my brain was starved of human interaction.

I decided that I wasn't going to awkwardly wait around for them to change into their shoes. I stepped onto the bouldering mat and eyed up the wall, looking for a nice, easy route to do first.

Feeling like I'd waited almost too long, I chalked my

hands and started climbing. When I was overly anxious or stressed, I have a tendency to overdo it when exercising. I could feel myself pushing those limits, not caring if I fell off or pushed myself so hard that I got hurt.

Tommy was the first to come in. He put his shoes on and tiptoed across the mat behind me.

I was in too much of a world of my own to be bothered by him staring. I reached the last hold and tapped it with both hands, letting out a grunt of success before I downclimbed. I jumped the last little bit and landed awkwardly on my feet. Tommy reached out to catch me, but the momentum knocked us both over. We lay there laughing for a moment before I looked up at him.

"I'm sorry, I was in my own world then."

"I could tell. You're pretty cute when you're concentrating."

"People usually describe it as terrifying, but I'll take *cute*."

He smiled warmly, not breaking the intense eye contact. For a split second, I thought he was going to kiss me. I saw it cross his mind, his eyes serious and hungry.

"Get a room," Jake called as he burst through the door.

I punched Tommy on the arm and rolled to my feet. I extended my hands to him, offering him help up. He took them and I pulled him to his feet. He was lighter than I expected, being so lean, causing me to pull him a little too hard. He stumbled a little but played it off as an excited little hop.

Thankfully, Skye and Jake headed straight for the rope climbing area instead of joining us on the bouldering wall. I didn't feel like making conversation with the stick-thin stranger.

We'd been there about an hour when Skye joined me by the bags as I was getting a drink.

"Hey."

"Hey, enjoying yourself?" I asked politely, taking a sip of my water.

"Yeah, it's fun! I'm so weak, though."

"Ah, you'll get stronger every time you come."

She nodded approvingly and took a swig of her diet coke. I tried to keep my emotions off my face.

"Gotta have my fix, I am low key addicted," she bragged.

"Worse things to be addicted to, I guess," I replied, thinking about how people were so blasé about drug users.

"Amen sister, my dad doesn't let me drink the stuff at home, so I make the most of it when I'm out."

"You live at home?"

"Yeah, my dad has a security firm, seriously protective, but he's minted so I don't mind."

I smiled politely and snapped the lid back on my water bottle.

"Back to it."

"You guys are so cute together."

"What?"

"You and Tommy."

"Oh, we aren't together."

"Sorry! But why the hell not?"

"I don't know, it's new and I kind of have residual feelings for my ex, it's complicated."

"Ooooh, dish?"

"I don't really think there's any dish, we broke up a month ago, and the other night we kinda kissed. We haven't spoken about it, but I don't know what... I am talking way too much, sorry."

"No, no, it's not too much! I get it, do you think that you and your ex are going to get back together?"

"There's a chance, but I don't know," I said carefully,

trying not to show how uncomfortable I was becoming.

I hated talking about my relationships with friends, never mind people that I'd only met that day.

"Well, it sounds to me like maybe it's time to let it go. Tommy is cute."

"Yeah, maybe you're right," I replied quietly, trying to keep my cool. "Anyway, talking of cute, you and Jake?"

"We aren't dating, just casually seeing each other."

"Ah, I see. Does he know that?"

"We've spoken about it," she said a little too defensively.

"What are you girls talking about?" Jake came barrelling towards us, a large grin on his face, sweat dripping from the tips of his short, fair hair. He slipped his arms around Skye's waist and gave her a kiss on the cheek.

I raised my eyebrows at her.

"Oh, nothing, you know, make- up, chick flicks, wine, that sort of thing..." I babbled, trying not to give enough detail that he'd ask further questions.

"Har har..." He untangled himself and leant over to grab his drink off the bench.

"Anyway," I was glad for the opportunity to leave.

I smiled politely and returned to Tommy and the wall.

"Hey!" Tommy smiled, sitting up from his sprawled position on the bouldering mat.

"Hey there," I smiled back, stretching enthusiastically.

"I couldn't help but overhear your conversation with Skye."

"Oh... I... what part?" I didn't know what to say, in case he didn't overhear the part were we were talking about him.

"The part about Dean."

"Look, Tommy, I... I don't know Skye well, and girls like to gossip. I didn't mean it."

"So, you didn't kiss the other night and you don't still have feelings for him?"

"No – I mean, yes, but it's not like that, it's complicated, and just that you and I aren't really..."

"*Aren't really* what?"

"Tommy, I'm going to go home."

"Yeah, okay, see ya."

I changed quickly and grabbed my things, not waiting to say goodbye to the others. I understood where he was coming from, but it wasn't an argument I was willing to have so soon. A red flag, for sure.

It didn't take me long to get back home, walking briskly in silence and replaying the two strange conversations in my head, wondering how I could have handled them better. Well, it was no use now. And it cannot be undone.

I threw my bag inside my room and stomped to the kitchen, not caring to look through the window for signs of activity.

"Hey," a rather flustered Caitlyn yelped as I crashed through the fire door.

"Hi," I replied defensively, intent on going about my business.

"You okay?"

"Wouldn't you like to know," I snapped.

"I'm trying to be nice."

"I find that hard to believe."

"Well, you won't even talk to me, so how am I supposed to explain?"

"You ignored me for months and now you want to talk? I don't have time for this right now."

I abandoned my tea making and returned to my room, leaving Caitlyn standing there with her mouth hanging open. I don't know what she expected, seeing me in that kind of mood. It didn't exactly invite conversation.

Normally, I might have engaged with her and tried to sort it out, but after what had been happening recently, I was at the end of my tether.

A soft knock came at my door several minutes later. I took a deep breath and crossed to the door, ready for round two.

There was no-one standing there. Instead, as I looked around, there was a steaming cup of tea on the ground by my feet.

I swore under my breath as I reached down to grab the mug.

"Thanks!" I shouted loudly, not knowing where she'd disappeared to. I closed the door and fumed silently.

I know it seemed like a nice act and something I shouldn't be annoyed about, but that's how they get you. On the surface, they're sweet and charming, but actually it's so they can poison you later on.

I sat back in my desk chair and checked my phone. A message from Dee and one from Tommy. I couldn't be bothered to open them, let alone reply, so I tossed the device aside.

Grief and guilt gripped me suddenly. If only I had messaged Nina back that day, then maybe she wouldn't have been driven to do what she did, if she'd had the chance to get whatever it was off her chest.

I was a bad friend.

I opened my phone again and checked the messages.

Dee: *Hey girl! I have the wine and Doritos, see you later x*

Tommy: *I'm sorry about earlier, can I make it up to you? Drinks tomorrow? Xx*

It didn't take me long to decide what to say to both. I tapped furiously for a minute and then returned my phone to the desk.

I drummed my fingers restlessly on the cheap, wooden desk, thinking about the events of the last few days. I pulled open the top draw and retrieved my diary. Time to unload.

I wrote for a solid hour. Getting every detail, every emotion I felt, every little thing that happened no matter how insignificant.

I slammed the book shut, feeling somewhat better. I would re-read it tomorrow to check if I' missed anything, but, for now, I just wanted to relax.

* * *

The doorbell rang at 10:39p.m. and I jumped up from my chair. I was disoriented for a moment, before realising that I'd fallen asleep. My sleep pattern had taken a hit in the last few days of laying low.

I charged into the hallway, wanting to beat Hugh and Danny to the door.

"Hey, babes," Dee greeted me, a Tesco bag in one hand and her satchel bouncing on the opposite hip.

"Come in, m'lady," I said, swinging the door wide and curtsying dramatically.

"Why, thank ya, my dear."

We stomped to the kitchen and laid out our bounty. I took out two large bowls for the crisps, and Dee raided Hugh's cupboard for glasses.

"You heard from Dean?" she asked, taking a deep swig of her wine.

"Not since the police station. Do you think he'll be okay?"

"He's going to be fine."

"He blames himself for Nina."

"It wasn't his fault, she made the choice. You don't think he's going to...?"

"I don't think so, he was upset the other day after she... but, he wasn't as hysterical as she was..."

"Matty? What is it?"

"I need to call Nick," I announced, pulling my phone out.

"Who the hell is Nick? We're talking about Dean. You know, the hunky blond with the dreamy blue eyes that follows you about?"

I ignored her and clicked on P.C. Nick Wilde's contact, praying for it to connect.

"Matty! Who's Nick!"

"P.C. Wilde, hi!" I said down the phone, shooting Dee a knowing glance. She stopped talking immediately and her face sunk into anxious attentiveness.

"Matty, what can I do for you?"

"I have a theory, can you meet me?"

"I shouldn't even be in contact with you, can't you tell me now?"

"Fine, but you have to promise that you won't think I'm crazy."

"I... sure."

"I think Nina killed Sarah, by accident. I think she tampered with her drink at the party during the game of shot roulette. I think that's why she killed herself."

"Matty, that's ..."

"Don't say crazy."

"I was going to say smart, it's more than the police have."

"There's more. I think that someone put her up to it. The guilt she felt about killing Sarah wasn't typical of your classic premeditated murderer. I want you to see if it's too late to do a toxicology on Sarah, see what was in her drink."

"So, not a tidy *blame it on the dead girl* situation. I'll see what I can do, but I'm suspended, and without probable cause I doubt they'll take it seriously."

"You'll have to give them enough to make them want to do the toxicology, but not enough that they'll ruin our work. No offence, but I don't want this case dead ended."

"None taken, but I'm only a P.C., and I'm suspended. How are we going to solve this?"

"You want to help me solve this?"

"Yes, Matty, I want to solve these deaths. Besides, I can't let you do it alone, can I? You'll get yourself killed."

"Fair point. But I thought you weren't even supposed to be in contact with me?" I added flirtatiously.

"Don't do anything stupid. I'll get back to you," he said before hanging up.

I sighed with satisfaction as I set my phone on the breakfast bar.

"Bloody hell, Matty."

I almost forgot Dee was there and tried to hide my surprised jolt. I looked at her with a mix of embarrassment and sadness.

"Two things – one, you totally have the hots for Detective Nicky. Two, if Nina felt so guilty about Sarah, does that mean she wasn't the intended target or that it wasn't meant to go that far?"

"Dee, what if it was for one of us?"

"Matty, you have to be careful. If you're right, then there's a murderer still out there and you don't want to get on their radar."

"I have Nick on board now, I'll be fine," I said as convincingly as I could muster.

"Alright," she sounded less worried. "Well, this wine won't drink itself!"

I smiled, trying not to seem too distracted or concerned as we took the wine through to the living room and continued our evening festivities.

* * *

I awaited a call from Nick for days before continuing to investigate. He should have known that I would plough on without him. I hoped that he hadn't told his superiors my theory. It would really annoy me if he sold me out and claimed my theory as his own. He could – I don't even know him that well.

I decided that the best plan of action was to go to the library. I could see if there was literature to back up my theory so that I knew I wasn't leading Nick on a wild goose chase that might cost him his job. I needed to see if Nina's behaviour was typical of someone who'd committed manslaughter. I also wanted to create a profile on our potential killer so that I had something to show Nick when he got back in touch.

I grabbed my laptop and notebook, stuffing my arms into my down jacket hastily. I threw my backpack onto my shoulders and crammed a singular AirPod into my left ear.

I was hoping that since it was so close to the end of the Christmas holidays that there wouldn't be anyone studying, and I'd have free rein of the facilities

It was exactly like I'd hoped. The library was empty. I went upstairs and secured a computer at the back, so even if someone did come in, I was nice and tucked out of the way.

I decided to do a computer search to see if there was anything useful that popped up straight away. To see if something signposted me to any books that we had here at the university. The library wasn't extensive because of the limited space, but the larger campuses allowed us to order books from them if we needed them. I wasn't going to use that feature today; I didn't have time to wait days for them to arrive.

I did a copious amount of reading before I was confident enough to write some vague notes.

A killer's profile – notes.

- *Major mental illness and previous violence.*
- *Instability in social relationships, or inability to maintain lasting relationships.*
- *Job instability.*
- *Antisocial, manipulative, and exploitative individuals.*
- *Psychopaths: no responsibility for the crimes.*
- *Being removed from a parent's care before the age of sixteen.*
- *Being subjected to cruelty or physical abuse by caregivers.*
- *Lacking a stable and supportive environment.*
- *Sadistic fantasies, intrusive homicidal thoughts, self-injury.*
- *Impulsiveness.*

Suicide – notes.
- *More than 700,000 people die due to suicide every year.*
- *A prior suicide attempt is an important risk factor for suicide.*
- *Suicide is the fourth leading cause of death among*

fifteen-nineteen year olds.

- *77% of global suicides occur in low- and middle-income countries.*
- *Ingestion of pesticides, hanging, and firearms are among the most common methods.*
- *Substance abuse.*
- *Mental health issues.*

Satisfied with my research and spurred on by *hangriness*, I decided to leave the library. I pulled out my phone and clicked on Nick's contact.

It rang for several moments before he finally picked it up.

"Hello, P.C. Wilde speaking," he answered, telling me that he wasn't in company that it was acceptable to be in contact with me.

"I need to talk to you, call me when you can talk."

"Wrong number, no worries, bye."

I hung up. I knew that he had to do and say those things, but it still stung. I put my AirPods in and turned the volume up on my *moody tunes* playlist.

It was late now, and the sky was dark and clear, the stars twinkling gently, the moon the main source of light on my journey home.

I couldn't help but think of the conversation I'd had with Dee about how I could be a prime target for the murderer. Especially since I was investigating the deaths. I walked faster.

I always hated walking through the shortcut from our estate to campus at night. It was a muddy woodland path that was pitch black and remote. Today was so much worse, my heart was pounding in my chest, and I cursed myself for walking alone so late, thinking about the last conversation I'd had with my Mum, promising her that I would be more careful.

I made it back to the house in record time, cramming my key in the door and looking over my shoulder like I was in a horror film... the killer could be right behind me.

I slammed the door shut behind me and shivered with relief.

"Matty?" a voice called from the kitchen.

"Hello?" I called back, dropping my bag and coat inside my bedroom before setting off to find the voice.

As I rounded the corner to the kitchen, I saw them. Jamie, Danny, and Dean were sitting on the stools by the breakfast bar.

"Hey guys, what's happening?" I asked, seeing the look of worry on each of their faces.

"Dee told us."

"Dee told you what?" I asked nonchalantly, understanding from the look on their faces what they were on about.

"What you said to P.C. Wilde on the phone the other day," Dean stated, his hard stare was cold as ice and boring right into my eyes.

"It's just a theory. Anyway, from the research I've done today I've managed to narrow it down. The murderer has been non-violent so far, strategic, and..." I stopped when I saw the expressions on their face shift from worry to outrage.

"Matty, this is insane! Non-violent! They are responsible for two deaths; we don't want you to be the third."

"I understand what you're saying, but there's a pattern here, and if this person isn't stopped then there are going to be more deaths!"

"But it's got nothing to do with you, just step off," Jamie added. I knew that once he got involved that it was serious.

He never usually got involved with group politics.

"It's got everything to do with me, though. This is literally what I am going to do for my career! It's great extra credit," I joked, trying to make light of the situation, and hoping they'd drop it.

"We just wanted to tell you how worried we are, and that from now on, you aren't leaving our sight."

"Seriously? I appreciate the concern guys, but I don't need babysitting." I smiled at them thankfully and headed back to my room, wanting to organise my notes.

Dean followed me.

"Matty, wait."

"Go away, Dean."

"I can't let anything happen to you... I couldn't save Nina. I won't let anything happen to you."

I turned to face Dean, his steely eyes softened.

"Nothing's going to happen to me, Dean. You don't have to worry about me."

"I do worry about you though, Matty. I don't want you to chase this."

"Thanks, Dean, but you don't get a say in what I do or don't do."

"So, you'll let Nick look after you but not me?"

"He's a police officer, Dean! It's his job to protect people."

"I'm sure that's the only reason," he said spitefully.

"What the hell is that supposed to mean?"

"Oh, come on, I saw you on the day of Sarah's memorial, basically throwing yourself at him."

"Screw you, Dean," I spat.

I slammed the door behind me and locked it. I slid my back down the soft wood on the inside of the door, not believing what had just happened. I tried to tell myself that it was jealousy of my not wanting to go back to him after he cheated on me, and dumped me, and then kissed me out of the blue.

I pulled out my phone and clicked on Tommy's contact.

Me: *Pub? X*

He responded almost immediately.

Tommy: *Meet you at* The Rule *in 30 mins? X*

Me: *See you then! X*

I put my phone back in my pocket and sniffled, edging away from the door that I knew Dean was still loitering behind.

In a classic *this is what you could have won* fashion, I changed my top, did my hair and make-up, and selected several pieces of jewellery before spritzing myself with enough perfume to be smelled through the door.

This routine took me about fifteen minutes, which was perfect because it meant I didn't have to wait, hiding anxiously in my room, before setting off to the pub.

I breezed past Dean in the hallway without saying a word. I went out the back door to where the bikes were stored before he could rise from his perch on the stairs and follow me. I unlocked my faithful, old, electric blue mountain bike and swung onto it without missing a beat.

I was off like a flash, there was no chance of being followed at the speed I was going. Although, I was aware of the loud clanging of the bike lock on the metal frame. Oh, and the lack of safety precautions I'd taken. Oh well, it was just a quick ride. What was the worst that could happen? Normally I would wear a helmet, but tonight I didn't have time to find it and wasn't willing to mess up my hair. Vain, I know.

I reached the beer garden at the back of *The Rule* in under five minutes. I locked the bike to one of the sturdier looking benches and fluffed my hair back up, not one for the windswept look. I made my way inside.

I breathed in the smell. The old pub smell of beer and crisps, and the damp of the passing walkers and their dogs, mixed with the sweltering heat of the log burning fire.

Knowing that Tommy wasn't going to arrive for a few more minutes, I went to the bar and scoped out the talent, knowing full well that I would order the same thing I usually did.

"A pint of Cascade please, Reggie," I ordered.

The barman and I had gotten to the point of being friendly, as it was my most frequented watering hole.

"Anything else?" he said, looking around to see who I'd come with.

"That's everything for now, tah, just waiting for a friend," I replied with a smile.

"Dean coming to meet you?"

"Dean and I aren't together anymore. I'm just meeting a climbing buddy."

"Ah, sorry to hear that. You made a good pair," he said, holding out the card machine so I could pay.

"Yeah, well, he cheated on me, so whatcha gonna do?"

"Crikey, sorry, Matty."

"It's fine, I try not to let it get to me, we're still friends. I never found out who it was, either."

"Oh, well, barmen can find out anything. I'm sure I've seen Dean come in here with a girl before, I can point her out to you when the opportunity arises, if you like?"

"Thanks," I said, laughing, not quite knowing if he was serious or not. He tapped the side of his nose and then ripped the card receipt off the device.

I turned around, clutching my pint, and walked into the room with the dart board and games machine; the room to the left of the bar as you walk in through the front door.

The room was empty despite it being dark outside. People around here didn't need an excuse to drink. They must all be on the other side of the pub, closer to the fire.

I made sure to sit facing the doorway and put a coaster over the top of my drink. It was safe to say that since Sarah's suspected poisoning, and the gang's concern that I might be next, I was a little bit more wary of my surroundings.

Tommy texted to say that he was on his way, and I relaxed.

I was content taking out all my frustrations about Dean and Nick on the battered dartboard. Was that why I was out with Tommy, despite the horrible argument we had at the climbing wall the other day? Was I just trying to prove something to Dean? Was I trying to prove my friends wrong by showing I didn't have a thing for Nick? Did I have a thing for Nick?

There was no time to find out because Tommy strode past the room and towards the bar. He ordered quickly and stuck his head around the corner to see where I was.

"Hey!" I said, seeing his cute boy band-esque face. I couldn't help but smile.

"Hi, Matty, I'll be through in a second," he said before disappearing back to the bar to collect his drink.

I fluffed my hair again, nervous that I had actually made an effort this time instead of letting him see me in my climbing gear, all sweaty and gross.

"I'm so glad you texted!" He put his drink down by mine. He leant in for a hug and I one armed him for fear of stabbing him with the remainder of the darts in my hand.

"Yeah, me too, I didn't want to end things like that."

"I was such a tool, I'm sorry."

"No, I get it. If anything, it's Dean that's the tool in this scenario. He's the one that kissed me despite me telling him I didn't want to get back together."

"Dean *is* such a tool. None of us like him, but that's because of the Skye thing. And I'm not a fan of how he cheated on you, either."

"What's the Skye thing?" I asked, suddenly hyper-fixated on that one nugget of new information.

"Well, Jake told us that Dean cheated on Skye when they were seeing each other. After he cheated on you. And he's ghosted her ever since."

"That's weird," I replied, not adding the part where I thought it didn't sound like Dean at all. Which then put me onto the questions the police were asking about him, how he was there when both girls died, and... no, it couldn't be Dean, right? He felt so guilty about Nina, and I doubted he would want anyone dead. But most people are charmed by serial killers and that's how they get away with it for so long. People are like, "No it couldn't possibly be so-and-so, they're so nice!"

"He's a scumbag," he said strongly, putting his arm around my shoulders protectively as I shrunk inward. "Plus, she doesn't like her photos being put on social media, or so Jake says. She's a very private person. I think Dean was too obsessive."

I took a slug of my pint and thought back on my time with Dean. He never showed any red flags while we were dating, and even though Lily and Dee didn't really like him, they were CrimPsyche too and were in a better position to pick up on things like that. Come to think of it, I blocked Dean on social media after he dumped me, so there was no way I would have seen any pictures he posted with Skye. Lily would have, and she would have told me right away. So, was Tommy misinformed, or was Lily trying to protect me?

"You okay?" Tommy asked, worry plastered on his angelic features. He was concerned he'd offended me by feeling so strongly against my ex.

"Yeah, just trying to piece a few things together."

"Anything I can help with?"

I thought about telling Tommy everything about the deaths, and the case I was building on the suspect. But he had proven himself to be the gossiping type. I didn't want to inadvertently tip off the suspect that I was onto them; people had warned me that that would not end well. But, then again, maybe I did want to tip them off? If the suspect was flustered into thinking that someone was onto them, then they might get sloppy and try and make a move. I wasn't a fan of the idea of using myself as bait, but if I was right and the murderer was someone I knew then maybe I had no choice.

I told him everything, aware that we were in a public place and could possibly be overheard, and that he could go away and tell everyone. Aware that he was also present at the party where Sarah was most-likely poisoned, and at the memorial where Nina was compelled into taking her own life. Not that I thought Tommy was capable of murder, but then again, he got me doubting Dean. So, anyone was in the running at this point, weren't they?

He sat there in silence for a moment after I had finished, digesting the seriousness of what he'd heard. Several times he looked like he was going to say something. You could see the cogs grinding about in his pretty head, but he stopped himself and thought some more.

"I'm going to go to the toilet. If you wanna run away because you think I'm batcrap crazy, then now is the time to do that," I joked, punching him lightly on the arm as I rose from my seat.

When I passed the bar on my way to the toilet, business had picked up and I was surprised no-one had come to join Tommy and I in the games room.

My trip to the toilet was uneventful, just the way I like it. On my way back, I decided to pass the bar and order another drink before it got too busy.

When I got back to the table, Tommy was gone. I huffed with regret. Was I stupid to think that he would stay after hearing my crazy theory? I was contemplating the consequences of my actions when I saw his jacket draped over the back of the bench we'd occupied. The sickening feeling in the pit of my stomach subsided. He hadn't left. Or he had left, and was in so much of a hurry to get away from me that he left his jacket on a cold January evening.

I sat back at the table and tried to wipe the anxious emotions off my face, taking several deep swigs of my pint, waiting for Tommy to return.

"I thought you'd actually ran away." A smile cracked my face. I took a sip of my drink playfully as he ambled back into the room.

"I'd be a fool," he replied, sliding onto the bench beside me. Then came another one of those moments were I thought he was going to kiss me. He looked from my eyes to my lips and bit his lip indecisively. I had the sense that he wasn't going to make the first move.

"Kiss me," I heard myself say. Whether it was brought on by the alcohol, or the fact that he had listened intently to my ramblings without running for the hills, I can't say. But I knew that, in that moment, it's what I wanted.

He didn't hesitate then. His climbing-calloused hand

wound its way through my hair, pulling me closer. His lips were soft and gentle – even though he had been desperate to kiss me, he didn't rush.

It was unlike my kiss with Dean, which had been sudden, hard, and intense, making me breathless. Tommy was sweet, tantalisingly gentle, making me take the lead.

I closed my eyes and pressed myself into him, ignoring the sounds of the pub beyond.

"God, get a room!" a voice interrupted from the doorway.

Pushing myself away from Tommy like two teenagers caught doing things they shouldn't be, I opened my eyes and snapped my head towards the sound.

"Jake," I said as a greeting.

"Matty," he replied, smiling mischievously and giving Tommy a knowing look that said, *"It's about time,"* and, *"Dude, nice,"* simultaneously.

I inadvertently slid a few centimetres away from Tommy, giving him an embarrassed smile. He squeezed my hand and returned my smile. It was like a secret, something the two of us had shared, something sweet, pure.

"You gonna hang in the doorway or are you coming in?" Tommy asked Jake.

"Vampires have to be invited over the threshold to come in," I quipped before Jake had the opportunity to open his mouth.

He feigned being stabbed in the heart and made a small choking sound.

"You wound me, Darcy. Nah, I'm just waiting for Skye at the bar," Jake answered, ducking out of the room and throwing his jumper around his shoulders like a middle-aged golfer.

I turned to Tommy. He was already looking at me.

"That was nice," I admitted, cocking my head to one side and smirking.

"Very nice," he said, putting his arm around me again and leaning forwards. His eyes had that sexy intensity to them, the look you could always see coming. The kind of look that made butterflies jump and somersault in my stomach.

Tommy patted his jeans pocket, feeling the familiar shape of his mobile phone missing. He reached over and checked his jacket, with no luck.

"Have you seen my phone?" he asked me, concern turning his cheeks pink.

"No, did you take it to the bathroom with you?"

"I don't think so."

"Well, you had it on the way down because you texted me, it has to be in the pub somewhere, maybe go check the bar?"

"Yeah, I'll go check now."

Just as he was rising off the bench, a figure rounded the corner into the room, striding with purpose.

"Matty!" the figure called from the doorway. The speaker sounded a mixture of shocked and enraged. I turned around expecting to see another one of Tommy's friends.

"Dean?" Tommy and I said at the same time.

"What the hell are you playing at?" Dean accused, stomping into the room. I stood up and held my hand out in front of me, a globally recognised stop sign. He ignored it and pushed me aside roughly.

"What the hell, Dean?" I squeaked.

"This guy! Sends me a picture of the two of you with your tongues in each other's mouths, and you're asking me what the hell?"

"What are you on about?"

94

"Yeah, got one of your little friends to do it, did you?" he spat, squaring up to Tommy.

"I have no idea what you're on about?" Tommy genuinely looked shocked. He patted his pockets down and came up empty, as proof of his innocence.

"See, he doesn't even have his phone," I interjected.

"Then who sent me that bloody picture?"

"Dean, you need to leave." I spoke with all the authority I could muster.

Jake and Skye came through the doorway. Their faces were a picture of confusion, seeing the three of us stood defensively in a triangle. It must have been quite the sight.

"This looks fun," Jake announced, taking a sip of beer.

"Not now, Jake," Tommy spoke softly, like he was dealing with a wild animal.

"I'll go," Dean responded, accepting defeat.

When he turned to face the exit, his face drained of all colour, and he looked down at his feet. Could it be because of what Tommy had told me earlier about him cheating on Skye, too? Did he feel more guilt about her than me? Or was it the fact that we both happened to be in the same room?

He pushed past Jake and Skye without another word. Very uncharacteristic of him.

"I'm going to go check on him, I'll be quick," I said, pecking Tommy on the cheek quickly before literally chasing after my ex.

I was interrupted by Reggie the barman on my way out. He was collecting glasses by the door when he said to me in a coarse whisper.

"That blonde haired chick that went into the games room a few minutes ago."

"What about her?"

"It's her."

"Thanks, Reggie, gotta run."

Confused about what exactly it meant, I ran out of the door and down the street, not knowing which way he'd decided to go. I saw the spark of a lighter in the distance and made my way towards the bench it came from.

"Care to explain?" I asked, plonking myself down on the bench beside him.

"Funny, I was going to ask you the same thing."

"I told you we weren't getting back together."

"And what about Detective Nicky?"

"I do not have a thing for P.C. Wilde!"

"Right."

"Right."

We sat in silence for a minute before Dean offered me a cigarette, I took it gratefully.

"You should go home, Dean. Get some rest."

"Are you saying I look tired, Darcy?"

"That is exactly what I'm saying."

"Fine."

"Can I ask you something first?"

"Anything," he replied. He looked so exhausted and defeated that I almost felt I was taking advantage of that.

"It was Skye, wasn't it?"

He took a deep breath before responding. Words failed him. He nodded guiltily.

"She lied to Tommy and Jake, that's why they hate you."

"What do you mean she lied?"

"She told them that she dated you and you cheated on her as well."

"Then how did you find out?"

"Tommy and Reggie, I put the pieces together."

"The barman?"

"Yup."

"Huh."

"Imagine cheating on your girlfriend in her favourite pub," I teased.

Dean looked hurt.

"I never meant to hurt you, she just... she's... look, it doesn't matter now, does it? I screwed up, you moved on."

"It's okay," I said, actually meaning it this time. After seeing everything that he'd been through, the emotional turmoil he felt about Skye and understanding what happened, it stripped me of the anger and resentment I'd felt for him.

I can't believe that there was a point in the night where I thought that Dean had hurt Sarah and Nina. That he was some kind of criminal mastermind hell-bent on causing chaos throughout campus.

"I better get going, leave you to your date."

"It's not..." I began, but it was impossible to deny. "Goodnight, Dean."

"Goodnight," he said as he stretched and began walking away from the bench into the heart of the village. He didn't look back.

I waited until I could no longer see him before sighing deeply, watching as the cloud of warm breath puffed from my mouth, through the air, and dissipated before my eyes.

I walked back to the pub and joined Tommy, Jake, and Skye at our table in the games room.

"Hey, sorry about that."

"You always have to go chasing after him, don't you?" Skye accused.

"Excuse me?"

"Can't you see he's just doing it for attention? You're lapping it up, leaving Tommy to sit here on his own, and wait for you to stop chasing after your ex."

"It's funny, I don't remember asking your opinion, Skye. In fact, I don't remember inviting you here tonight, either. You just show up, don't you? Like mould, never expected, never wanted, but really bloody hard to get rid of." I was angry now. The fact that she had the nerve to comment on my relationships when she had lied to and manipulated Jake and Dean. No doubt she was trying to do the same with Tommy.

"Jesus, Matty, calm the hell down." Jake stood up defensively.

"Sit down, Jake. It's about time Skye fought her own battles, don't you think? Oh, come on, don't get all quiet on me now. Nothing to say this time, Skye?"

"Come on, let's go," Jake said, pulling Skye by the arm and escorting her out of the pub like I was some kind of rabid animal that might attack at any moment. Skye was speechless. Her expression bewildered, like she didn't expect to be confronted, and didn't know how to deal with it.

"God," I said, sinking down into the bench with my head in my hands.

Tommy shifted uncomfortably beside me.

"Tommy, I'm so sorry, I didn't mean to snap."

"Honestly, I've never really liked Skye, and that was very hot."

I blushed uncontrollably before flashing him a flirty smirk.

"Oh, you thought that was hot, then just you wait."

He leaned over and kissed me again, this time with more urgency, more passion.

"Come on, let me walk you home."

"Did you ever find your phone?" I asked, suddenly remembering the reason crap hit the fan in the first place.

"Oh no, I didn't. I'll go take another look around."

"Ask Reggie to keep an eye out for it. We know that it was here because of the picture, which, what the actual hellas that all about?"

"I have no idea, but it looks like someone wanted to cause some drama. Although, I don't see what anyone stood to gain from any of it, no-one came out of this unhurt."

"That's true," I said, wondering if it could have been the murderer, trying to cause a rift. Or, that their next victim was in the room at some point. Jake, Tommy, Dean, and I were all at that game of shot roulette. It could be any one of us next. Time was ticking on the case. It couldn't be long before the murderer struck again.

"Do you want to stay over tonight?" I asked sheepishly. "I don't like the idea of you walking around at night with a murderer on the loose and no phone."

"Would you have asked me to stay over if you wasn't worried that I might be murdered?" he teased.

"Hard to say," I replied flirtatiously. "I'm just going to grab my bike, you go talk to Reggie and I'll see you out front?"

"Good plan." He gave me a peck on the cheek before exiting the room.

I waved goodnight to Reggie and wandered out the back, slipping my jacket on lazily.

My bike was exactly where I'd left it, thankfully. I entered the four-digit code and pulled the lock free, clipping it back in place once it was free from the bench.

I wheeled the bike to the front of the pub absentmindedly, thinking about the information I'd gathered that day and how I was going to turn it into a workable profile. How it would be a huge task to find the person behind all this chaos. How it was turning us all against each other.

Tommy was waiting for me at the front, his hands stuffed into his pockets coolly, stamping his feet rhythmically to counteract the fact he was wearing Converse on a freezing day.

"Ready to go?" I asked, reaching him, the bike wheels ticking along sadly beside me. "Did you find your phone?" I asked as an afterthought.

Tommy shook his head sadly. "Let's go." He linked his arm through my free one and we walked back up the hill to my estate, chatting the whole way.

The stars were out in full force now and it was possible to see each one; the sky was so clear and cloudless. It was going to be another cold night. Under different circumstances, I would be glad of the company.

PART THREE

TOMMY

13th January 2020

Dear Diary,

So much for my new year's resolutions. I've landed myself in an episode of *Midsomer Murders*. Not the experience I wanted for my future job, but I want to get to the bottom of it. (At least I'm sticking to my diary writing resolution). Sarah OD'd, Nina killed herself, and we have no idea why any of it is happening. I just hope if I keep writing down everything as it's happening then I'll start to build a bigger picture. If there is a bigger picture. There has to be.

I need to get Dean off my mind. Tommy can help me do that.

P.C. Nick Wilde is an interesting character; I can't work him out.

I awoke late the next morning. I yawned and stretched, careful not to interrupt Tommy's angelic sleeping body. He was like one of those Greek statues, chiselled expertly from marble. I smiled as I glanced over at him, watching him take calm, shallow breaths.

I grabbed my phone instinctively and checked the time, 10:19 a.m., and saw that I had several messages.

Dean: *Home safe, hope you're okay.*

Dee: *;)*

Nick: *Meet me at Daisy's at 10a.m.?*

I cursed and typed out a reply. Just as I was about to hit send, my phone started ringing.

"Hello?"

"Matty, thank god, are you coming to meet me?"

"I've just woke up, just read your text, I'll set off ASAP!"

"I'm right outside your house, I was worried something had happened to you."

"It's only been twenty minutes. Jesus, Nick, everybody knows I'm never on time for anything."

"I'm parked outside, see you soon." He hung up after a brief pause, as if he was debating saying something else.

I stared awestruck at my phone for a moment before placing it gently on the bedside table, not wanting to wake Tommy. I turned around to see him looking at me.

"Good morning! I'm sorry if I woke you."

"Good morning, it's okay, who was that?"

"P.C. Wilde, he's outside, I'm filling him in."

"Oooh, exciting," he murmured sleepily, struggling to keep his eyes open.

"It's 10:20a.m., so I was late, that's why he came to the house."

"It's 10:20? I'm late."

"Late for what?"

"Work!"

"Crap, I'm sorry!"

"It's alright, you didn't know," he said, jumping out of bed and pulling on his clothes from last night. Tommy worked at the clothing store underneath the climbing wall – a prestigious outdoor brand that he got sweet discounts on. It's the perfect job for a budding outdoorsman.

"You can borrow my bike, the code is 1066."

"Thanks! Also, the Battle of Hastings? That's a terrible code and you should seriously consider changing it.

Anybody with half a brain could guess that."

"Whatever."

I speedily dressed, brushed my teeth and hair, and washed my face, trying not to splash water down my clean top. I was ready before Tommy. I kissed him on the cheek and said a hurried goodbye.

Even though I knew Nick was waiting for me, I was shocked to see that there was a police car sitting outside. I walked over to the window and saw Nick sat behind the wheel. I opened the front passenger side door gingerly and stuck my head inside.

"Have you come to arrest me?" I asked sarcastically.

"Actually..." he began, his face devoid of all emotion. I must have opened my eyes wide with surprise because he laughed. "Just get in."

I slid into the seat and turned to face him.

"So?" I asked, gesturing around the interior of the police car.

"I've been reinstated, my suspension is over."

"That wasn't long."

"Nope, I think they knew that I wouldn't leave the case alone."

"Great! So, we have access to police records and resources!"

"I have access to police records and resources. You aren't attached to this case in any legitimate capacity whatsoever."

"Fine," I huffed. "Can we still go for breakfast? I'm starving."

"Of course!"

We drove to the café and sat down in the corner next to the window. It wasn't very busy as it was one of the coldest days of the year and tourists were less inclined to visit Ambleside. The months after the start of the year were always the quietest. People were skint from Christmas and didn't have money to waste on taking trips.

The windows had steamed up, so it was hard to see outside. It didn't matter too much as there was little footfall. Anyway, it was better if people couldn't see me meeting with a police officer in broad daylight.

We waited for our full English breakfasts to arrive before talking about the case.

I explained everything I could without showing him the notes and the articles I'd collected, for worry that they would get food on them, and that he would think I'd gone completely crazy.

"I'm not going to lie, this is really impressive," he said. Once our plates had been cleared, he asked to see the notes and the vague profile I'd come up with.

I flushed with pride.

"So, you think it had to be someone at the party?" P.C. Wilde asked.

"Yes, otherwise they wouldn't have had the opportunity to spike the roulette, but that someone would have had to have something on Nina. It couldn't be someone random either, it had to be a student or someone who knew a lot about student life and our peers, specifically. And then again, at Sarah's memorial, I didn't see anyone out of the ordinary, so it has to be someone known to us."

"Okay, and you still think they aren't finished? That they are trying to kill someone who was present at the roulette game?"

"I do, and I know that two is just a coincidence, but do we want to wait until there is a third?"

"No, we don't, but like you said, it is completely circumstantial and coincidental at the moment. So, what do we do now?"

"I want to search the police records to see if there's any

history of mysterious deaths in the pasts of these people," I said, sliding a list of names across the table.

"There are a lot of people here."

"I know. It's everyone I've confirmed was at the party. I also want to get the security footage from the memorial and cross-reference whether they were at both. Can we get access to Nina's phone records to see if there's any suspicious activity there?"

"Jesus, Matty, you'd make one hell of a detective."

"Can you do it?"

"Yes, but it's a long process, I need warrants and probable cause to get access to either."

"Great."

"Is that all?"

"Actually, there is one more thing," I added with a mischievous look on my face.

I explained to Nick what had happened last night at the pub with Tommy's phone going missing. About there being another circumstance where there were several of the potential targets in one room.

I asked him if there was anything he could do to get the phone back, or to see who took it, or where it might be now. Anything that might point us in the direction of who took it – because I had a strong suspicion that it was linked to the murders, and that the intended target was in the room last night.

"Matty, you need to be more careful. If I thought I was the intended target I would have my head down. Not be stirring the pot and meeting with bloody police officers in broad daylight."

"Am I trying to goad the killer a little bit? Yes. Am I being careful? Also, yes."

"I could order surveillance on your house, just in case."

"If it makes you feel better," I replied, knowing that it

was the sensible option. My friends and family would go ape if they knew I turned down that sort of protection, given the circumstances.

"Done. In the meantime, you don't go anywhere alone. If you need anything, just give me a call."

"Alright."

"I'm serious, Matty."

"I know, thank you."

"Now, time to get to work. What are you going to be doing while I work my way through this list?"

"The less you know the better."

"Matty..."

"I'm just going to do some light stalking. I have a friend who does computer science..."

"Okay! Okay! Enough, I get it. Just know that any evidence you collect illegally won't be admissible in the court of law."

"I know, that's why you're getting evidence legally."

"Fine, just—"

"Be careful," I interrupted with a smirk.

"Exactly," he said, trying to hide a smile of his own.

We heard the sirens of several ambulances race up the high street, and the wail of police and fire services was unmistakable in the background – how could we have missed that? We jumped up from our table, glad that we had paid when we ordered, and tore out of the café. I stuffed the notes back into my tote bag messily before I raced after Nick.

The noise was coming from the mini roundabout near campus, a few hundred yards from the café.

My heart sunk with dread as we pounded closer. Nick was wearing his uniform, so they let him past the quickly assembled taped area. I was stopped from getting any closer. Nick gave me an apologetic look and left me behind.

From what I could see, there had been a multi-vehicle collision. The fire service were cutting open cars and dousing the flames while the police were still cordoning off the crash at a safe distance, redirecting traffic and pedestrians in the process.

I was ushered further back after being asked to leave and being informed that they couldn't tell me what had happened or who was involved. The whole roundabout was now a crime scene. I had to walk back into the heart of the village, through a shortcut, and up the back way to the campus just to get a better look.

I sent Nick a text message for him to reply to whenever he next looked at his phone.

From my perch at the top of the car park, behind some bushes, I had a better view of the incident than when I was stood on the roadside.

I could see four mangled cars and several bloody, shaken people being pulled to the side of the road and wrapped in blankets. A large white tent was erected over the centre of the crash – no doubt the cause of the whole accident.

I squinted my eyes to see what was going on under there. I couldn't make out a body, although I guessed there must have been one in there by the reaction of the police, and the fact that they were covering it up.

I saw a knotted piece of metal jutting out of the front of a silver Škoda, something that looked like it could have been a bike frame.

My heart stopped. I recognised that bike frame. Electric blue. That was my bike. Which meant that. The. Body. Was. Tommy's.

* * *

Life went on. How dare it.

* * *

I don't remember much of what happened in the days following Tommy's death. There was another police interview, another memorial – Nina's, another period of isolation. I hadn't left the house since. Lily and Dee were with me 24/7. Whether that's under Nick's instruction or not, I don't know.

Days were spent moping around like an anti-ghost; physically present, but mentally far away. Nights were spent sleepless and shaking, thinking morbidly about the fragility of life. I couldn't get my head around it. He was here that morning, lying in my bed with his perfectly chiselled features. Warm and passionate. Now, nothing. Blink and you missed it.

I wanted to believe that it was over, that Tommy was the final stop on the murder express, but there was too much doubt prickling my restless mind. Doubt that seethed. It was your bike, it should have been you, if you had died that night at the party, then Sarah, Nina, and Tommy would still be here. But I couldn't work out why.

I don't remember voicing my opinions to Nick or my friends, but I must have, because they were all trying to convince me that none of it was my fault.

PART FOUR

MATTY

15th January 2020

Dear Diary,
What's the point?

I don't know what snapped me out of my funk, but it happened at the most bizarre time.

Nick had come over with the cross-referenced list of people at both the party and Sarah's memorial. He told me there were too many factors surrounding Tommy's death, with it being so public. It was impossible to place anyone there, especially since there was a twelve hour window in which the bike could have been tampered with. I did suggest that they should get forensics on the bike to look for prints or any DNA that the killer might have left behind. Apparently, there was too much interference from the crime scene for them to get solid evidence.

"I've put a star against the people that were at both," Nick said.

I scanned the list. Out of what must be around a hundred names, there were twenty or so possible matches. That fact alone made me sick. That so many people who were in attendance at the party but didn't want to say goodbye to Sarah perplexed me. Then again, many of that number would be people who attended the memorial but not the party, which made me feel a little bit better.

"Have you looked into their backgrounds?"

"I can't, apparently it's not relevant."

"It's relevant to match it to the profile of the murderer!" I complained. Not at Nick directly, but at the hoops the police must jump through to keep everything ethical.

"I know it's frustrating, but data protection is serious."

"I know, I'm sorry, I'm just so tired. I want this to be

over."

"Soon," he said. His eyes glazed over with seriousness as his thoughts transported him elsewhere.

It was clear that the case had taken its toll on him, too. I can't imagine how helpless he felt every time another body dropped. Especially since we were so close to saving Nina. Then, there was the fact that I was potentially the intended target for the crash. That was something I tried not to dwell on – that Tommy was collateral damage in some serial killer's scheme.

We were sitting on the huge corner couch in my living room, close enough to feel the warmth of each other's bodies. I put my hand on his shoulder and gave it a reassuring squeeze.

"We'll get through this, Nick."

"Welcome back," he said, smiling sadly, covering my hand with his shovel sized one.

"What?" I replied confusedly.

"This is the most you've spoken since... and you have that mischievous glint in your eye again."

"Well, we have a murderer to catch."

* * *

That night we laid out all the information we had so far, along with the information my computer scientist friend was able to collect. We managed to strike a few names off the list, using location data and social media posts as alibis. We managed to half the list of suspects. Ten down, ten to go!

"Happy 2a.m.!" Nick slurred sleepily.

"Crap!"

"I should go home," he said, stretching and sliding off the stool animatedly.

"You can stay, if you like," I said, not realising how it sounded.

"Matty..." he began.

"On the settee! You can stay on the settee!" I blurted, trying not to turn bright red at the embarrassment of propositioning a police officer.

He laughed warmly.

"It's fine, if I stayed then people would start to gossip," he said, raising his eyebrows insinuatingly.

"Yeah, good shout."

"I'll text you later," he said as he put on his coat and boots and headed for the door.

"Goodnight, Nick."

"Night, Matty."

I watched him walk down the corridor without looking back, and only when I heard the soft click of the door shutting behind him did I relax. I cursed myself for being so inactive and so unbelievably naïve when it came to Nick.

I scooped up the papers and my laptop and took them back to my room, depositing them safely in the middle drawer of my desk. I slammed the drawer shut and flopped onto my bed. I fell asleep instantly.

* * *

I must have made a habit of not locking my door, because when I awoke Dee was sitting on the edge of my bed with a cup of coffee and a plate with two slices of toast.

"Good morning," I murmured, sniffing deeply the delicious morning smells.

"Good morning, sleepy head," she cooed like a mother hen.

I sat up in bed and accepted the offerings gratefully.

Dee smirked.

"What?" I asked, between bites of heavenly buttered toast.

"Nick told us you were doing better. And I see it," she said, smiling, tears pricking the corners of her eyes.

"Oh, Dee," I squeezed her arm, willing her not to cry, because if she cried then so would I.

"It was so scary seeing you like that."

"I'm so sorry Dee, it won't happen again, I'm here now."

"I don't expect you to stop chasing his killer. If you need anything, I will help you end that prick."

"Thanks, babe, I love you."

"I love you too, dummy."

"Wait, you talked to Nick?"

"Yeah, he stopped by before his shift."

"Weird."

Dee made a *hmm* noise and proceeded to ignore my comment. I tried not to overthink his visit, but I couldn't help myself. Was it weird that I'd never met the guy before these murders started? That he had access to so much information and resources. That people tended to trust, be honest with, and do anything a police officer asked of them?

Was I paranoid? Perhaps. But was I on to something? Probably not. I texted my computer scientist friend, just in case. I wanted to know more about P.C. Nick Wilde.

I slurped down the rest of my coffee and tried not to wait for my phone to chime.

"Fancy going for a walk?" I asked Dee out of the blue.

"Hell yes, girl," she beamed, slapping her thigh excitedly.

* * *

We decided to walk to Rydal Water, a body of water 2.3 miles away from Ambleside. We always took the back road that skirted underneath Loughrigg Fell. The views were amazing, and even though it was still technically a road there were hardly any cars that drove on it.

My body was stiff and aching by the time we plonked ourselves down by the water's edge. I cursed my lack of inactivity. We pulled out flasks of tea and some sandwiches we'd picked up from Tesco.

We sat enjoying the crisp winter air, the picnic, and the comfortable silence.

* * *

We were back an hour and a half after we set off. It wasn't a long walk, but we dawdled and spent some time gazing wistfully across the water's mirror-still surface.

I put my key in the door and swung it open, feeling relaxed and refreshed after our jaunt into nature.

"Matty?"

"Hello?"

I rounded the corner and saw the rest of the gang crammed into the living room like sardines, music blaring. They were unable to tear their gaze from the screen, where an intense fight was occurring. They mashed buttons on their controllers, seemingly at random.

Lily was the only one who greeted me properly. She rose from the floor and threw her arms around my midriff.

"Hey, dude," I said, returning the pressure despite the height difference.

"Save me from these boys," she whispered into my shoulder.

"Ha-ha, okay, come on, kitchen."

I took her hand, led her out of the room and down the

corridor. The boys hardly even realised. They were too engrossed in their game.

Dee went straight for the wine and poured out three generous glasses, not even stopping to strip off her outer layers from our walk.

I took off my coat and hung it over the back of a chair.

"I can't believe you left me here! With them!" Lily pouted, nodding her head vigorously towards the living room.

"Sorry, it was a spontaneous thing," Dee explained, handing out the wine.

"Cheers," we chanted in unison before chugging from our glasses.

Afternoon drinking slowly turned into a sesh, and before we knew it, we were at the pub. Again.

Dean met us there after I drunk texted him. He hadn't been around much since Tommy's death.

* * *

The night passed quickly, mainly because we were drunk when we arrived. We actually left the pub considerably more sober.

The four of us decided to grab some food on our way home. The only place that was open so late was the new takeaway place near Tesco.

We ordered and stood outside waiting, barely aware of the cold but thankful that the rain staved off.

The conversation was stilted. Both girls were wary of Dean and what I had told them in some sort of depressed, paranoid state. They couldn't help but think that he was capable of murder. Maybe they were right. I had been wrong about him so many times before. But there was nothing in the profile that pointed towards him. He didn't even have a motive, and he was so cut up when Nina killed herself, but that could have just been for show.

I was driving myself crazy with impossible scenarios, being unreasonably paranoid.

Thankfully, Dean didn't seem to notice the girls giving him the cold shoulder. He was more focussed on tiptoeing around me, trying not to trigger anything that would remind me of Tommy. He never said it, but it was obvious. He was never usually so filtered.

The food was ready. After we picked it up, we wandered to Dee's place because it was closest and crammed around her small kitchen table, savouring our greasy takeaways.

"Are you coming back with me?" I asked Dee as she unbuttoned her jeans and slunk lower in her chair.

She groaned sleepily.

"I guess that's no, then," I chuckled, looking over to Lily who was looking very tired and deflated.

"I live around the corner, I'm going to go to sleep in my own bed without the sweaty, farting, clingy man-child."

"That's fair."

"Aaaaah," Dee groaned again.

"Right, into bed, c'mon," I said, taking her by the arm and dragging her to her bedroom door. Lily and Dean followed gratefully.

She bade everyone goodnight and slunk inside.

I looked at the other two and we exchanged a furtive glance.

After leaving Dee's, Dean and I watched Lily go over the street to her house. She waved at us from the other side of the road.

"So, what are your plans?" I asked Dean.

"Let's just walk."

"Fine," I responded. We started walking in the

direction of my house.

"I feel like I need to apologise."

"What for?"

"For not being there for you when you needed me."

"Dean, it's fine."

"I don't know how to make you trust me again."

"Be my friend," I whispered. "Be there for me when I need you. Answer the phone when I call you crying about some other guy, walk me home when I'm drunk."

"I can do that," he promised, smiling, and sniffling suspiciously.

"Thanks."

"Come on, let's get you home."

"Actually, I need some time to think, on my own. I'm not that drunk, don't worry."

"Is this a friendship test?" he whispered with a huge grin on his face.

"No, this isn't a friendship test," I laughed heartily, returning his infectious smile.

"Okay, because if you text me later and fail me for not being more persistent about walking you home, I'll egg your car."

"I give you full permission to, in that case."

"Okay, goodnight, Matty."

"Goodnight Dean."

He turned and walked away, stuffing his hands into his black peacoat pockets to stave off the winter chill. I watched him for a few more seconds, wondering whether I had made the wrong decision of just wanting to be friends.

I didn't have time to think for long because soon he was gone and I was standing, alone, in the middle of an empty street staring into the distance like a loony.

I breathed in the bitterly cold air, feeling freer than I had in weeks. Maybe it was the alcohol, but I was really glad in that moment that I wasn't being babysat or observed for signs of mental fatigue.

I turned just in time to see a hooded figure sprinting towards me from the side street. Normally, this wouldn't worry me. It was just some guy out for a really intense late-night run. But, after three of my peers had been murdered, I didn't know anymore.

As the runner got closer, I noticed that they were wearing a balaclava, and I started to panic. No-one innocent went running at night wearing a balaclava.

They were barely three feet in front of me, and I seriously expected them to slow down. To pull out a weapon and mug me. But that didn't happen.

They pushed me. Using their full weight, coupled with the momentum from their downhill sprint.

I felt myself catapulted backwards. At first, I thought that the low wall would catch me, but the momentum slammed me into it, and then sent me somersaulting over it. The drop into the river from that point would vary depending on the time of year. Because it was winter, and it had hardly rained, the river was dramatically low, barely a trickle in some places. The drop would have easily been twelve feet from the top of the wall to the riverbed.

I screamed. I felt it rip through my body with such ferocity I'd never be able to recreate. Luckily, the momentum kept me spinning on my way down otherwise I would have landed on my head, and that would have been it.

I landed with a sickening slap, on my back, and my head hit solid rock. The freezing cold water below numbed the pain. I was knocked unconscious immediately, unaware of whether my attacker had stopped to see the end result, or whether they had fled, unaware of my body fighting the shock of the cold water and the trauma of the impact.

I was as good as dead, there was no doubt about that. The chances of someone finding me in time were slim, and even if I was conscious enough and able to call for help, there would be no guarantee I could be saved. Sarah couldn't be. Nina couldn't be.

Tommy couldn't be.

I couldn't tell whether I was drifting in and out of consciousness, or whether I was having some bizarre out of body experience. Then, I heard the slapping of footsteps on tarmac. I hoped it wasn't my attacker coming back to finish me off.

Someone was shouting, calling out. I tried to make my body move, but it wouldn't do anything. I couldn't open my eyes. I couldn't shout for help. I wanted to cry, but I couldn't do that either. Someone had heard my scream and was coming to investigate, but there was no chance they would think to look down here.

I was resigned to my fate, slipping back to unconsciousness.

The next noise I heard was my phone ringing in my pocket, something that never happened. Usually it was on silent, but the fall must have knocked the 'do not disturb' button. I was grateful, but also unsure how much time had passed since I heard the shouting. It couldn't have been too long, otherwise I would have frozen to death.

My phone continued to ring, I heard footsteps coming back, someone shouting again. Would they look over the wall? Would they hear the ringing? It was too much, the pain was too much.

I passed out again.

* * *

I opened my eyes to see white all around me, blinding white light that made me wince. I squinted to allow my eyes to adjust to their new surroundings. Was I dead? Was this the light at the end of the tunnel they always talked about?

Slowly, things began to come into focus. The sharpness of the light sent a blinding pain through my head, forcing me to close my eyes again. I took a deep breath and gritted my teeth.

"She's waking up," a voice beside me announced, ringing and echoing in my ears unnaturally.

I felt a flush of warmth go through my arm and the pain in my head subsided. I opened my eyes. My head felt woozy, and my body felt really light, like it was made of clouds. I giggled.

"Is she okay?"

"We just gave her some strong painkillers, she'll be fine, but not exactly with it."

"Thank you," said the voice that I couldn't place.

I looked around the room. Everything was white – but only because I was in a hospital, I realised. I tried to move my head but stopped when I felt resistance. I looked down, using only my eyes. My neck was restricted by an unattractively beige brace. The rest of my body was cloaked in a hospital gown, but without further restrictions. Nothing else was broken. I was somewhat relieved.

"I..." My voice sounded weird, slurred like I was drunk, but also like I was underwater. I tried again, really focussing on the words I wanted to say. "I'm not dead."

"No, you're not dead," they responded gently. I still didn't recognise the voice through the distortion. With my vision impaired, I wasn't able to see the speaker clearly, either.

"Why?" I asked. It sounded more philosophical than I

meant it. Not in a 'death is not the worst that can happen to men' way, but more of a 'fill in the gaps of my memory' kind of way.

"Someone heard you scream, went looking for you. It's funny, they nearly gave up, but then they heard your phone ringing and, well, the rest is history."

"Who was it? That found me." I closed my eyes again, feeling the painkillers working their magic on my battered vessel.

"It was someone on their way home that night."

"You say 'that night' like it wasn't yesterday."

"It wasn't yesterday, Matty."

That sentence filled me with such panic that, if I wasn't so high on painkillers, would have given me a heart attack. I knew what I was going to have to ask next, but actually saying the words meant that I would get an answer, and I wasn't so sure that I wanted to hear it. What if it was weeks, months, years ago? What if I'd left my life behind and everyone has moved on without me? I felt the tears burn my eyes as they rose to my ducts.

"How long ago?" I asked, opening my eyes and bracing myself for the answer.

The speaker was about to respond when someone came knocking on the door.

"The doctor will be along shortly to run some tests on Miss Darcy."

"Thank you."

I turned my body slightly to see the man sitting in the chair beside my hospital bed.

"Nick."

"You remember my name," he said, leaning forward, smiling hopefully.

"Like it was yesterday," I laughed painfully. Clutching my ribs didn't help the pain ricocheting through my body, but it was useful to know that my arms were still functioning.

"Maybe less of the dark humour. You've been asleep for seventeen days." He studied my face for a reaction, holding his breath in case he'd caused me more emotional turmoil.

I relaxed. I smiled.

"Thank you," I gushed.

That's when I really looked at him. He wasn't wearing his police uniform, which meant he wasn't here on official police business, but in his own free time. He was young, maybe in his early to mid-twenties. It was hard to place because of his serious expression. His eyes were a sparkling blue – not like Dean's, his were paler. His dark hair curled messily over his forehead, unlike the day I first met him when it was slicked back and smart.

"Hey, can I ask you something? And you have to promise me you won't be offended," I asked.

"Sure, ask away."

"Why are you here? You aren't in uniform, so I'm guessing it's not for work."

"I am not here for work, no."

"So, it's because you're a creepy guy who has a thing for coma girls?"

"Funnily enough, it's not that, either."

"Then, what?"

"It was me."

"What was you?"

"I found you."

His face changed, from smiling and relieved to serious and reminiscent.

He found me. That's why he's here. He was the one who found my battered and broken body lying in the river that night. He must have been scared crapless, like I was with Sarah. It brought back memories of seeing Nina's and Tommy's lifeless bodies.

I remembered a few days ago – or weeks ago, I guess – when I asked my friend to do some digging on Nick, and I felt stupid. How could someone so pure and sweet be capable of murder? He is the one that saved me, after all, which should in itself clear him of any suspicions I had.

"Nick, I..." I started. What was I going to say to that? I didn't know? I'm sorry?

"It's alright, you're alright."

"You saved me," I said, looking at him intensely. Without this man, I would be dead. "I owe you, big time."

"You don't owe me anything, I don't want you to think that's why I'm here. My job is to protect people, and besides, I couldn't have the deaths of four students on my patch in one semester. That would be crazy." He tried to make it sound like he was upbeat, not creepy at all, and definitely coping healthily. A strange mix that doesn't complement each other well.

"Well, that's too bad, because I'm now obligated to follow you around forever, swooning and holding up signs that say 'I heart P.C. Wilde', like the little green aliens from *Toy Story*," I joked, throwing a hand up and smirking.

"Very funny," he laughed. It was nice to see him smile and look so relaxed. It was obvious that the past seventeen days had taken their toll on the young policeman. I almost felt guilty, until I remembered that I was pushed and didn't simply fall.

"Did they catch whoever pushed me?" I asked suddenly.

"What do you mean, pushed you? It wasn't an accident?" Nick was alert now, his posture rigid and his eyes sharp.

That's when the doctor chose to come in to do the tests.

"Good afternoon, Matilda! So happy to see you're awake. We need to do some tests now, nothing too invasive, don't worry. But we will need some privacy, officer."

"I... sure thing. I'm going to make a phone call. I'll be back soon." He looked from the doctor to me, nodding intensely as if he needed to reassure me that he wasn't abandoning me. That he was on the case.

"Take your time, son. You've spent more time here than I have, recently. Why don't you go home and get some rest, a nice shower, some food that isn't from the hospital cafeteria?"

"Sure thing, Doc, after I sort out this tiny new lead, I promise!" he called from the doorway as he rocked anxiously from foot to foot.

"Right! Let's look at you then, shall we?"

* * *

The tests took longer than I had patience for. Some were to check brain function and memory, others were for movement and my physical well-being.

I was distracted. Worried. About what Nick had said about not knowing I'd been pushed. Did people think that I'd fallen over the wall and into the river? Or worse, did they think that I'd jumped? That I chose to end my life the same way Nina did? Well, not the same way Nina did, but...

With the support of the doctor and a nurse, I was able to walk slowly around the room, which, I was told, was a positive sign of recovery. They said they didn't want to risk taking my neck brace off just yet, as they didn't think my neck was ready. They said I was lucky it was just a sprain. I bit back my sarcastic response about the word 'lucky'.

As the nurse was clearing up after the doctor, I asked her an abundance of questions.

"Without sounding like a classic clichéd student, can I ask, do you know what happened to my phone?"

"Oh sweetie, you can ask me anything, and don't worry, I don't judge! You didn't come in with one. I guess it must have been seized by the police or something."

"That's weird, if they thought I fell why would they seize my phone?"

"I don't know, sweetheart."

"Sorry, I... another one. Did the hospital contact my Dad? He's my emergency contact."

"That, I do know. Your parents were both here for two days when you first came in. Then, your Dad went back home to work, and your Mum comes every morning, she booked into a hotel just down the street."

"Okay, cool, thank you."

"And your friends stop by every evening, like clockwork. The busiest visitor log in the whole hospital," she said, beaming proudly.

So, they hadn't moved on without me. Granted, it had only been seventeen days, but still, my heart soared. I tried not to think about the other side of that coin, the 'how long would it take them to stop coming' side? To move on with their lives? To give up hope?

"Thank you, Nurse Kelly."

"My pleasure."

She finished up and left the room quietly, flashing me a sweet smile as she closed the door.

I looked up at the large, clinical looking clock on the wall opposite my bed which read 3:12p.m. My friends wouldn't be here for another few hours, at least. That is, if

Nick hadn't told them that I was awake yet, in which case they would be here much sooner. But something about his reaction earlier made me think that he was probably wanting the police to talk to me before anyone else.

Without my phone I felt lost. I wasn't able to scroll mindlessly through social media, watch Netflix, or read a book I'd downloaded to take my mind of things until my friends arrived. Too much time to think was always a bad idea for me; I was a serial over-thinker.

I decided that I would have to do something else to take my mind off it all. I pulled back the covers and shimmied to the edge of the bed. The hospital gown riding up my thighs was the least of my concerns. The sooner I could be back to normal, the better.

My friends joked that I was the Queen of Burnout, because I worked and studied so hard. But the honest truth of it was that I couldn't actually sit still. I always had to be doing something.

I dangled my feet over the edge, smiling again at the thick socks my mother must have crammed onto my feet, because she knew how cold I always was. And how I hated to sleep barefoot. I felt guilty that I couldn't tell her I was awake.

That was when a thought hit me; I wasn't too young to remember a time before mobile phones. I could just call her off a landline. Good thing the doctor wasn't here to see that revelation, otherwise my brain test results might have taken a hit.

I let my feet touch the ground. It felt nice to be in control again, even if my body simultaneously screamed with pain and ached like a hell.

I stayed close to the bed, because I felt like I needed something to lean on, and felt my way to the door, using various other pieces of furniture as my walking aids on the way. When I reached the door I opened it triumphantly, like it was all a part of my great escape.

On the other side of the door was a brilliantly white, clean corridor lined with assorted medical equipment on wheels, dumped there because the hospital seriously lacked innovative storage solutions.

I looked left and then right, trying to decide which way the reception was most likely to be.

I remembered when I was in hospital once, I was like eleven, and above my bed there was a TV that swung down and attached to it was a corded telephone. I damned modern technology.

The arrows on the floor led me to believe that the reception would be to the left, if subconscious conditioning could be believed.

I couldn't help but feel like I was going to get in so much trouble for leaving my bed, but it was kind of exhilarating.

The nurse at the reception desk looked surprised to see me, I'd even go as far as to say horrified.

"Good afternoon, can I use your phone?"

"You should be in bed."

"I know but I need to call my Mum, let her know that I'm alright."

"I can do that for you."

"She'll want to hear my voice."

She looked like she was going to continue to fight me, but she sighed and gave in.

"Fine, but then I'm taking you back."

"Deal," I said gratefully as I shimmied behind the desk and took a seat beside the nurse. She continued to tap away at her keyboard in order to trick my brain into thinking she wasn't going to eavesdrop.

I pressed each number carefully, after repeating the

number under my breath several times before I was sure it was right. I held the receiver up to my ear, praying that I got the correct number.

"Hello?"

"Mum?"

"Matty?"

"Mum, it's me, I'm okay."

"Oh, thank god..."

"I just wanted to call you and let you know that I'm alive. I'm sorry for scaring you."

"...You stupid girl, what you go and fall in a river for, anyway? Your father and I always warned you about being safe around water while drinking."

"Mum, stop, please. I don't need to hear this right now."

"You're right, I'm glad you're okay, honey. I'll come over as soon as I can."

"Oh, Mum you don't need to do that, you've been here once already today."

"To stare at my comatose daughter, yes, but I need to see you now."

"Okay, see you soon. I love you."

"I love you too, bye."

I put the receiver down and sighed.

"Tough cookie, your mamma."

"Yeah," I breathed.

"C'mon then Houdini, let's go."

I smiled and let the older woman put her arm around me supportively and walk me back to my room.

"Thank you."

"Don't mention it, seriously, I don't want people thinking I can't keep track of my patients."

I laughed, not knowing whether she was joking, but grateful, nonetheless. She tucked me back into bed and then gave me a stern look followed by a cheeky smile and a shake of her head as she closed the door, telling me the look was a joke.

I decided that I needed a nap. After all my mischief making and the physical exertion, I felt like I deserved it.

* * *

I awoke to find my room full of people. I blinked to make sure I wasn't hallucinating. I wasn't.

"Good morning," I croaked.

Everyone's heads snapped to look at me.

Everyone included: my Mum, Nick, Dee, Lily, Danny, Hugh, Jamie, Dean, and Sgt. Grumpy, aka P.S. McNally.

"She is alive," Hugh beamed sarcastically to break the tension.

They all fussed over me, asking me how I felt and filling me in with what I'd missed.

Eventually Sgt. Grumpy snapped. "Right, that's enough, yes we are glad she's awake, but we need to interview her while it's still fresh."

My Mum looked like she thought assaulting a police officer seemed like a good life choice.

"It's okay, let's get it over and done with," I shouted above the murmurings, and fixed my Mum with a sharp glare that convinced her to back off.

"Thank you, Miss Darcy."

Everyone bar Nick and Sgt. Grumpy left.

"Right, Miss Darcy. I have a series of questions to ask you, do you mind if this conversation is recorded?"

"No, I don't mind."

"P.C. Wilde."

Nick hurried over after making sure the door was closed properly and took a seat beside my bed. He set up what I assumed was a police issue tablet and pressed the red recording button. He gave the thumbs-up to signal its readiness.

"Interview on the 8th February 2020 following the incident of the night of the 21st January 2020 with Matilda Darcy, officers P.S. Roger McNally and P.C. Nicholas Wilde.

"Miss Darcy, can you tell us, in your own words, what you told P.C. Wilde earlier today when you woke up from your coma?"

"I asked P.C. Wilde if the police had caught the person who pushed me."

"Can you tell us what you remember from the night of the 21st January 2020?"

"My friends and I went to the pub, *The Golden Rule.* We left there when it closed around twelve. Dean and I walked Dee, sorry, Dean Walker and I walked Denise Davis and Lily Firth back to their houses before walking back along Rydal Road to go to mine."

"Sorry to interrupt, but can you tell us about the nature of your relationship with Mr Walker?"

"Dean is my ex-boyfriend and current friend."

"Why didn't Mr Walker walk you home like he did for Miss Davis and Miss Firth?"

"Because I asked him not to."

"Did you have an argument with Mr Walker that night?"

"Yes... no, it wasn't exactly an argument... I-"

"Have you ever thought Mr Walker was capable of hurting you, Miss Darcy?"

"What? No, of course not! You think Dean pushed me?"

"He was the last person to see you that night-"

"Nick, you agree with this?"

"In most of these cases, it is the boyfriend, husband, or ex responsible," Nick replied.

"Screw facts, tell me what you think."

"We are still building up a picture of what happened that night, we are pursuing several different possibilities."

"That is such a bullcrap answer, up until a few hours ago you all thought I jumped."

"And that line of questioning isn't off the table, Miss Darcy," P.S. McNally said, looking me dead in the eye.

"Fine. No, I don't think Dean is capable of doing something like that. Anyway, I saw him walk away. My attacker came from a different direction, from the road by *The Rule.*"

"Okay, tell us what happened after Mr Walker left."

"I watched him leave, watched him disappear around the corner by the bakery. Then I turned, ready to continue walking home, when I saw them. They came sprinting down the road, wearing a hoodie and a balaclava. At first, I thought they were out for a run, and then they came right towards me. My second thought was that I was going to get mugged, but they didn't stop running. They pushed me, I screamed, I fell, I hit the ground, and everything went black."

"You say 'them' when referring to your attacker; why?"

"I couldn't see whether they were male or female, also I guess I didn't want to assume their pronouns. Which sounds stupid since they tried to kill me, I don't know."

"Any idea of their height? Build? Anything you remember is useful."

"About my height, athletic, I guess, but it's winter so people layer, they weren't very strong."

"Why do you say that?"

"Because they used the momentum from the run to knock me over. I didn't feel like they would have been able to push me over without it, it's just a feeling I have."

"That's okay, we will get that information over to our e-fit guy and see what he can come up with. We will also cross-reference it with local CCTV footage from that night and see if we find anything."

"My phone rang."

"Pardon?"

"P.C. Wilde heard it and that's how he knew where I was, who was calling me so late? What happened to my phone?"

"That's right, your phone did ring. It got water damage, so we sent it off to be fixed, for when you woke up." P.S McNally stated, trying not to let us see his more human side.

"That's optimistic."

"We had to be," said Nick.

"Okay, you asked who called you, well, we won't know until we have permission to access your call history. We genuinely think it would help the investigation move forward."

"Yes. I give you permission to access my call history and anything else you need, locations, internet history, bank card transactions, anything."

"Thank you, Miss Darcy. That is very helpful."

"Anything else you would like to ask us?" Nick asked hopefully, his eyes shining sweetly.

"No."

"This interview is concluded. If new evidence comes to light and we require further information, we will contact you directly to organise an interview at the police station. Thank you, Miss Darcy, for your cooperation with this matter."

Nick switched off the recording and handed the tablet to P.S. McNally, who stuffed it into a huge pocket in his vest.

I tried not to look at Nick as he left, following P.S. McNally like a puppy.

I heard muttered voices in the hall before everyone came filing back in, their faces no longer excited, but serious and worried.

"Someone pushed you?" My Mum screeched like she was accusing me.

"Yes... I–"

"Why didn't you tell me? You let me believe you fell into the bloody river because you were rat-arsed."

"I didn't want you to worry."

"Well, I am bloody worried."

"Stop shouting, go get a coffee and calm down." My head was splitting, the headache I'd woken up with had only got progressively worse the longer I was awake. I covered my eyes with my hand as if blocking out the light and squeezing my face would make the pain go away.

"Are you in pain? Do you want me to get a nurse? Your father is going to kill Dean for the danger he's put you in!"

"I want you to be quiet," I snapped.

"Okay, I'll get a nurse," she whispered, patting my other hand lovingly.

"That woman," I said bitterly once she'd gone.

"She cares about you," Dee said.

"She's suffocating me," I responded, taking my hand away from my face and daring to open my eyes.

"We've all been so worried about you, Matty," Lily added almost defensively.

"Yeah, the police just told us they want to question us all again, for you," Dean mentioned, ignoring the comment my Mum had made about my Dad killing him. I'd honestly forgotten he was there until he opened his mouth. He looked drained, like being awake was almost too much for him.

"We had no idea you were pushed," Hugh said. His intentions were noble, but the comment annoyed me.

"You didn't all seriously think I jumped though, did you?" I accused, looking from face to face.

"We didn't know what happened," Hugh answered, looking venomously at Dean.

"You've been very quiet," I aimed at Dean.

Everyone turned to look at him as if they too had the same realisation.

"I didn't bloody push her!" he exclaimed.

"I know you didn't," I said, suddenly feeling very tired. "He didn't do it."

"Fine, but he shouldn't have left you alone," Hugh said, folding his arms and shrugging passively.

"I asked him to."

"Still."

"Can we please stop arguing? Talk to me about Uni, tell me everything," I said, closing my eyes and leaning back against the pillows, only half-listening to the words coming from my friends' mouths.

* * *

It was early morning when I woke again. The room was dark, but I could tell that dawn was fast approaching. There wasn't enough light to see the clock on the wall, but I knew.

I stretched carefully. It was going to take some getting used to, wearing the neck brace. I'd always hated sleeping on my back. I fumbled with the light switch on the lamp beside the bed, struggling to find it in the darkness.

The room filled with light, The tiny lamp was powerful

and bright, its white rays filling almost every inch of the room, chasing the shadows away.

I looked around the room. What startled me wasn't the sleeping figure sitting in the chair beside my bed. It was who the sleeping figure was that shocked me.

I hadn't been making much noise before, but I felt my body stiffen, not wanting to disturb the slumber of my sleeping guardian.

Nick had come back. After how annoyed I was with him at the interview, I thought he'd stay away. He looked so peaceful, so much younger than he did while awake, like all the stress just melted away.

I watched him for a while, the way his chest rose and fell steadily, thinking about why he had come back, and wondering if this was a regular occurrence or if he'd started doing it because he'd found out I was pushed.

He opened his eyes and saw me watching him.

He smiled. "And you said I was the creepy one."

"I mean, you are lurking in a chair beside my bed."

"Good morning," he replied, unfurling his body with a satisfying stretch. "How are you feeling?"

"Good morning, P.C. Wilde. I'm okay, how are you?"

"I'm fine, thanks."

"Nick?"

"Yes?"

"You haven't been sleeping here every night, have you?"

"Not *every* night."

"Nick..."

"But, not in a creepy way! I just couldn't bear it if you'd died. I saw how losing the others affected you and, I don't know, I just knew you had to be protected, at all costs."

"It shouldn't be a cost to you, though. You're a police officer. This is so much more than what's expected of you."

"I can't explain it."

I nodded sympathetically and kept my mouth shut. I was glad he was there and didn't want to drive him away again.

So, we just sat there in silence for a while.

* * *

I was allowed to leave the hospital after a few more days of tests and rest. I even managed to convince my Mum to go home after Nick promised he'd look out for me and gave her his personal phone number.

Dee and Lily spent more time staying with Hugh and Jamie at our house so that they could look in on me. They even made sure I got to my lectures on time and carried my laptop bag so I wouldn't strain my neck.

I was annoyed that I missed the first couple of weeks of Uni, but I was told I could have extensions on all my work for the rest of the semester due to the extenuating circumstance of being attacked and suffering a head injury. So, I wasn't worried that I'd fail my modules.

It did mean that I couldn't go back to work for at least another six weeks, or until I got my neck brace off and was deemed fit to work. So, I used the holiday days I'd saved up to ensure I'd still have income, once again annoyed that zero hour contracts don't entitle you to sick pay.

My phone chimed, bringing me back to the present moment. I made a disgruntled sound and put my phone face down on the sofa, glad that Nick had brought me my phone back so that I could receive such pointless emails.

"That Dean?" Hugh asked, unconvincingly unbothered.

"No, I haven't heard from him since the hospital."

"Prick."

"Go easy on him."

"Why?"

I didn't have a good enough reason so I remained silent, wishing I could shrug in response, but finding that many of my sassy responses were being impeded by my newest neck accessory.

I pulled up Dean's contact and closed it immediately. I shouldn't have to be the one to contact him. But I wanted to. I felt guilty for the guilt he was feeling about that night.

Me: *Hey friend, I did promise you could egg my car.*

Even though I didn't want to be the one to extend an olive branch, I felt like Dean needed some help. I smiled at the poetic justice.

Dean: *Damn, I'm all out of eggs! Rain check?*

I sent back an umbrella emoji.

A notification flashed across the top of my screen. An email blast on my University email. Intrigued, I clicked it.

It was some kind of gossip article, published under the alias Dr E. No doubt a nod to the omniscient presence of the optometrist's billboard in *The Great Gatsby*. Some people thought they were so bloody clever.

"Crap!" I gasped as I stared at the tiny rectangle of blinding light in front of me.

"Matty, what is it? What's wrong?" Hugh sat up, suddenly worried.

I thrust the phone at him without saying a word, just closing my eyes and leaning my head back against the wall, trying to steady my breathing. Trying not to think of the words I'd written in private, my inner thoughts, my scathing recollections.

"Damn, Matty, how did they get your diary?"

"I have no idea! I've been in the hospital!" I snapped agitatedly. I began drumming my fingers on my knees, trying to come up with a solution.

"You have to call Nick," Danny stated, cool as a cucumber.

"What? Are you crazy?" I replied, nearly in full panic mode.

"Someone broke into our house, Matty, stole your private property, and posted it online without your consent." Danny brandished my phone before me like it was going to solve all my problems.

"Well, when you put it like that," I replied, taking the phone, and clicking on Nick's contact.

He answered right away.

"Nick, I need your help."

"I've seen it already, don't worry, we are trying to take it down."

"Can you work out where it came from?"

"We can try."

"Thanks."

"Look, I've got to go, it's busy down here at the station, but I'll come by later?"

"Alright, yeah, see you later," I replied softly, glad that he was on my side. Concerned that he hadn't understood the implications of what was written in those pages.

The line went dead, and I continued to cradle the device to my ear.

"Now, damage control," Danny stated. Ever the cool headed one.

I groaned.

"What else was in that diary that could be used against you?" Danny asked.

"Literally everything," I responded, head in my hands.

"Okay, so damage control isn't possible then. When was it posted?"

"Just now."

"And someone wouldn't want to post it from their own personal computer, would they? Unless they had some serious security, and who has that?"

"To the library!"

"To the library!" he echoed.

Hugh, Danny, and I pulled on our shoes and raced to campus.

After barely a few metres I was out of breath. My body was bursting with pain, but I pressed on, lagging behind my two friends who were sprinting full pelt towards the library. I cursed my bruised and battered body.

Hugh got to the librarian's desk before Danny and I.

"Can you tell me if anyone has left the library in the last half an hour?" he panted.

Danny ran straight past him and went to check the study rooms on the ground floor.

Hugh was grilling the librarian, telling him of the incident that had occurred and the thought that the article was published right under his nose. I walked around the corner to the two rows of computers.

It hadn't looked like anyone had been on them recently, the monitors were all dark and the chairs were cold. I wondered what I would have done if someone had been sat there, had admitted to it. I pushed the thought away. It wasn't over yet, there were still more rooms to check.

Danny beat me to it and ran up the stairs, not having any luck in the study rooms. Hugh was still frustratedly trying to convince the librarian.

I followed Danny, knowing that the maze of

bookshelves up-stairs could hide more than you'd think. It would be easy to slip past someone who was looking for you.

I remember one night last year when Danny and I were up late writing our assignments. We were the only ones in the whole library, apart from the security guard that kept doing the rounds. We worked out that the lights were on motion sensors. So, in our self-allocated breaks, we would play a game were we had to sneak from one side of the library to the other without triggering the sensors. It was hilarious, and we barely ever managed to complete our mission, but it was still fun to try.

In a similar fashion to the game, we both took a side of the library and walked stride in stride, occasionally glancing at each other down the aisles, checking to see if there was anyone browsing the shelves.

We passed the middle, where there was a singular row of computers facing each other. All empty. We pressed on, growing increasingly more nervous after each passing shelf row.

Silently, we reached the end of the library, where the last of the computers were.

There wasn't anyone there.

I looked at Danny. I don't know whether I felt relieved or disappointed.

We skulked back downstairs to see if Hugh had made better progress.

He hadn't.

I texted Nick and told him of our suspicions. He said he'd look into it if the location data came back suggesting that the library was, in fact, where it was uploaded. But they couldn't act on the hunch of three mischievous undergraduate students.

We made our way back to the house, less agitated than

when we'd left, glad that we had tried to do something, even if it hadn't worked out.

* * *

Nick came over several hours later. He rapped on the door with a heavy hand.

I answered the door in my joggers and a sweatshirt.

"Hey, Nicky."

"Don't call me that," he answered, barely containing his grin.

"Come in."

Nick followed me to the living room where we sat on the huge corner sofa. It looked like he was going to say something important and then changed his mind.

"What is it, Nick?"

"We couldn't find where the article was posted from, we missed our chance to catch the killer."

"Nick... I... it's not necessarily the killer that posted the article, but I like the commitment to the cause."

"It's likely, though, that whoever pushed you, and who killed Tommy, Nina and Sarah, also broke into your house and posted your diary online."

"I guess it fits with the non-violent crime and manipulative technique we know the killer to have."

"I'm so sorry, Matty." He sounded annoyed and disappointed at himself.

"Nick, it's okay. I wasn't expecting you to solve the case single-handedly when I asked for your help, but we're so close, I can feel it," I gushed, leaning into him and squeezing his arm.

It was hard to keep the feelings down, that people had been inside every crevice of my mind, seeing all my deepest darkest secrets. That Nick had too. And Dean...

He looked at me looking at him and blushed. I leaned back again, removing my hand from his bicep. His eyes darted from mine to the ground, before a frown settled on his youthful forehead.

"So, the case," I ventured.

"You said the killer had a non-violent side? What do you mean by that? Three people have died."

"Yes, but the first was poison, the second was coercion, and the third was sabotage. None of them, up until their attack on me, was particularly aggressive in nature."

"So, what does that tell you?"

"That it's a woman, most likely."

"And the motive?"

"Usually some kind of gain, whether that's romantic or financial."

"So, our killer is likely a..."

"Jealous woman," I concluded.

"Which narrows it down a bit."

I paused for a second before responding.

"You have to arrest Dean."

"What on earth are you on about, Matty?" Nick exclaimed.

"It's just a hunch, but I think it centres around him. Nina tried to tell him something at the memorial, something she needed to get off her chest. The killer got him to show up to the pub, putting Dean, Skye, and myself in the same room. All this tells me that their motives are jealousy derived. That, and the fact that he's at the heart of this and nothing bad has happened to him yet. Which means that he either is the murderer, the next target, or the motive."

"So, why didn't they just poison Dean's drink at the party?"

"Maybe she got spooked, I don't know. I just know that

my drink and Sarah's were clear."

"Wait, what was that about the drinks at the party?" Nick asked.

"Sarah's drink was clear. I don't know what it was, but we didn't get to choose what we shot. It was just random," I responded.

"Okay, so let's think about this logically. There were eleven players, three of them are dead. That leaves Jake, Sol, Dee, Lily, Ryan, Katie, Dean and you as the intended target," Nick theorised.

"We can probably rule out Ryan, Katie, and Sol, as they don't seem to have had any trouble since then," I added.

Nick paused thoughtfully, trying to tie together the information in front of him.

"I'm the only one who's had trouble since then," I said jokily.

"But it could have been Dean that they were after the night you were pushed. You were together for a while; they could have got you by accident," Nick replied.

"I guess, so you're saying the target is me or Dean?"

"It seems a more viable theory than any of the others."

"What about my diary?"

"Who knows why they did that. You did smack talk Dean in the entry that was published. Maybe it was to taint his image."

"That is so specific, yet I can't think of why. I need the girls."

I rang the group chat with Dee and Lily and asked them both to come over. They obliged.

Within half an hour we were all sat around the table drawing up a spider map of all the possible enemies I had made during my time at Uni, and a separate list for Dean, sipping beers conspiratorially — apart from Nick, who refrained, trying to keep up the pretence of professionalism. Of course, I was biased, and didn't think that anyone really hated me, but thanks to my two closest girlfriends I had a full page of them by the end of the night!

"Right, wow, Matty," Nick sat back and looked at the finished piece. "You're a horrible person."

"Okay, whatever, get in line," I snapped back sarcastically.

We were then able to eliminate a fair few names from the last list Nick and I had made, the one based on whether or not they were at both the party and the memorial. This left us with several names of girls at our University that we knew had a thing for Dean, and were at both events.

These were the ones that we decided to go for first.

We spent another whole night plotting, scheming, stalking, and researching, and we still couldn't come up with a viable suspect. Nick focussed on his own theories, paying us little heed.

We ended up enlisting the boys – Hugh, Jamie, and Danny – to help us, since they already knew all the stories and were present at many of them. They could pass judgement and add commentary that we surely missed.

This only sought to increase our suspect list, not to diminish it like we planned. They came up with other potential suspects from other gossip that they'd heard and not cared to share with the group before now. Honestly, I was offended.

It was then that I decided that it was time to go to bed. There was no point trying to continue the case so exhausted and unable to think straight. I bade good night to everyone and headed to my room.

Footsteps quickened in the corridor behind me. I spun

around just as the fire door crashed shut. Nick was jogging towards me.

"Thought it was about time I left," he explained.

"Yeah, you weirdo, spending so much time in student houses."

"You know I'm only twenty-five, don't you?"

"So old," I teased.

"Careful," he teased back.

"Or what, you'll arrest me?" I dared, eyes wide.

He pushed me against the wall, flirtatiously, softly, towering over me by at least half a foot. He leaned down to whisper in my ear. I could smell a hint of alcohol on his breath, from the beers that Hugh popped open to, and I quote, 'help with the investigation'. The beer that he declined at first but couldn't help taking when Hugh offered, seeing the fun everyone else was having.

"See you tomorrow."

I groaned and let him push himself away.

PART FIVE

SKYE

13th February 2020

Dear Diary,

Sarah OD'd, Nina killed herself, Tommy was sabotaged, I was pushed.

A pattern emerges. But, what? How are we all connected? I am certain Dean is at the centre of it all, but it just doesn't make sense. Arresting Dean would draw out the mastermind behind, but we don't have a reason other than that. Not enough evidence.

Nick and I are working together, his police connection is really helpful, but I don't know how we are going to catch them.

It feels weird writing in my diary since it was leaked. Someone left the original in my room but uploaded the pages online, which meant they had to have had access to my room in the first place. Our door is always open, and with most student houses there are always people about. So, I didn't know for sure. But I had a hunch.

It had been nearly a week since Nick and I talked about arresting Dean. His boss wasn't so keen on the idea, despite the evidence we had collected so far linking the killer to my ex-boyfriend. And despite how legally we had acquired it.

There wasn't anything else we could do in the meantime, either. It was the next logical step in the plan.

Arrest Dean, see who kicks off, trace the leaked diary, catch the killer.

Easy-peasy.

I hadn't heard from Dean in a while. I was trying to

keep him at arm's length since the hospital. My theory surrounded him, and I'd nearly been killed. I think it's fair to say that I was feeling a little bit off him at the moment.

Plus, Nick warned me that telling Dean was a bad idea, that we had to keep him in the dark. I was worried about how that would make Dean feel, but I checked myself – better annoyed than dead.

I kept myself at home most of the time, unless I was with a group of my friends, with Nick, or attending lectures. If our theory was correct and someone had been trying to kill Dean all year but had only succeeded in killing three of our peers, they weren't likely to stop anytime soon. No-one who was present at the roulette game was safe.

I wanted to go climbing, but no-one thought it was a good idea since I was still wearing my neck brace. I couldn't help but agree with them, but I still wanted to do something.

I wandered around the bottom floor of the house, waiting for someone to come into the communal area. Danny had been spending a lot of time working on his dissertation, and his sleeping pattern was flipped so I knew he'd be asleep. Hugh and Dee had gone away for the weekend to see Hugh's family; I felt their absence on the bottom floor. Hugh's room was usually social with music playing, snacks going, and games raging at all hours of the day. Looking at the locked door made me sad for a time in the future when I knew we wouldn't be living together. Jamie and Lily were working.

I made a cup of tea and scrolled through the numerous social media apps on my phone, seeing post after post of memories with Sarah, Nina, and Tommy. I was drawn in.

There'd been several news reports on the deaths and countless theories, each more insane than the last. Some mentioned me and my friends by name, but others were vaguer; clickbait and puff pieces.

It's so easy to get drawn into the black hole that is social media. I must have scrolled through hundreds of posts, looking at the photos, absentmindedly cross-referencing the people online with the list again, in case I'd missed anything. That's when I saw something interesting that Jake posted.

It was several photographs of him and Tommy over the course of their friendship. One of them was at the party where Sarah was spiked. This itself wasn't what grabbed my attention, it was who else was in the photo.

Skye.

She wasn't on my list as being at the party. She didn't say anything about it either time we met, and I definitely don't remember seeing her there. Up until now, I hadn't thought of her as a threat, more like an annoyance.

She was at the party? So what? I know I'm only fixating on her because of the argument we had in the pub the night before Tommy died riding my bike. My bike, which had been chained up behind the pub we were all in. Could she have? No. I pushed Skye out of my thoughts, but not before I texted Nick with my new discovery.

Who was I kidding? I couldn't let it go. I trudged through all my notes again, finding out who had been in contact with who, at which event. I even contacted my computer science friend and asked him what he could dig up on her. I wondered why I hadn't done it before, shouldn't I want to know who my boyfriend had cheated on me with? And how could she make him so scared of telling the truth? I'd been so sucked into the mystery of Sarah's death that I let all this slide. That was so unlike me.

Nick replied more or less straight away with his idea of

a calming response.

Nick: *Don't do anything crazy, I'm on my way.*

I made a sound similar to that of a tyre suddenly expelling air and slid his message away. I continued to stalk Skye on social media until the doorbell rang half an hour later.

"Matty," Nick greeted, pushing the door open further.

"Nicky," I answered, moving aside so he could come in out of the drizzle.

He wiped his boots on the mat and shook tiny droplets of rainwater out of his dark hair.

"She did a stellar job making sure she didn't appear on social media the night of the party." I dived right in, not waiting for him to take off his boots or jacket. "I only found her because of the memorial posts people had posted. Jake posted a picture from the party; she was in it."

"We need to speak to Jake and establish an alibi for Skye so that you can drop this jealous ex thing."

"Excuse me?"

"Dean cheated on you with Skye, you want Dean arrested and Skye dragged over the coals. Don't think I don't see this for what it is, Matty."

"And what is this, Nick?"

"A personal vendetta." He turned and looked at me now with annoyance in his eyes. They looked more grey than blue in the dimly lit hallway.

"You're upset with me?" I asked, taking a step back.

"I thought you were serious about this case! I thought you were different, not just some pathetic student who only thinks about boys!"

"That's how you see me?" I asked, trying to stop the tears from springing free of their lash prison. I balled my fists. "You should go, Nick."

"No, I'm just saying how it looks. I can't be seen humouring you when it looks like a personal vendetta." Nick put up his hands in surrender, his face suddenly empathetic.

"But, what if I'm right?"

"What if you're wrong?"

"What do you want me to say, Nick? Oh, yeah, actually it could be me, I could be the killer. Is that what you want me to say?"

"What the actual hell, Matty? No, that's not what I want you to say. But I think you are being a bit naïve. Why would I think it's you?"

"You're being a bit naïve, Nicky, so invested that you can't see how close I am to it all," I said.

"Touché," he said, biting his lip and trying not to get annoyed. "I get it, okay."

"People can think what they want, but it won't matter when we catch the monster," I breathed, on the brink of tears.

Nick nodded, the wet curls on his head bobbing hypnotically with each movement.

"I can't do anything until you arrest Dean."

"I can't do that."

"I understand."

"Don't do anything stupid," he begged, his eyes sharp.

"I can't promise that," I replied, tears tracing soft lines down my face.

Nick looked like he was going to say something else but stopped himself. He shook his head and lowered his eyes to the ground to avoid looking at my tears.

I waited.

He stood brooding for a moment longer before storming away, leaving me confused.

The door opened roughly and then shut a moment later. Nick was gone, taking his feelings of resentment and anger with him.

With too much adrenaline buzzing in me to do anything else, I went back into the kitchen and paced around for a while, trying to release the energy.

* * *

I stalked Skye's online profiles, screenshotting and making notes. I Googled her name, trying to find out anything I could about her past since my computer science guy hadn't got back to me yet.

She was so careful. There was barely anything to look through and I was done within a couple of hours of starting. It was scarily clean. Would it be too much to assume that she changed her name to come to University? Her profiles were fairly new, but she'd explained that away in a post:

Old account got hacked so I had to make a new one aghhhhh! Add me!

Several people liked it, but there were no comments underneath. If it were my friends discovering that I'd had to make a new account because I'd been hacked, then there'd be lots of comments underneath detailing how stupid I was and how it was typical, or an older relative asking whether it was actually me.

I kept on trawling, looking through some of her Facebook friends just in case they had her old account friended.

I wasn't sure I'd find anything. I felt guilty and weird, like I was peeking through her windows and rifling through her drawers. I was so close to giving up, so close to forgiving Skye for being so unnecessarily shady.

And then I saw it.

On about the hundredth profile I clicked on, I saw her in the featured photos. Photos that Lisa Fletcher chose to pin to the top of her profile for everyone to see, even though they weren't the most recent.

I clicked on the photo of a younger Skye with darker, brown hair. Dammit, I should have known she couldn't have naturally been that blonde! I was excited now, knowing that I'd stumbled across something that might help the case, or something that might help me understand the enigma that was Skye Matthews.

I clicked through the names tagged on the photograph, none of them were Skye. I felt my stomach sink. What if I found something incriminating?

I clicked on each profile until I found out Skye's real name, her real profile. I took a deep breath as I scrolled. She'd kept updating the profile alongside the one we all had her on. That was shady, did she think that no-one would find it? It wasn't very well protected, so she mustn't have. Why did she say she'd been hacked?

I found a treasure trove of information. I carefully screenshotted and documented it, knowing that web pages could be taken down in an instant, and it was something so trivial that could ruin all the work I'd done.

Skye Matthews was actually Emma Seaton, adopted at age nine when she was orphaned after a house fire. She was a horse lover, a cosplayer, a local, and an only child. She changed her name before coming to University so that she could have a clean slate from her harrowed past while staying close to her adopted parents.

I Googled her real name and found all the articles pertaining to her parents' fatal demise. No wonder she was a ghost on campus. If she grew up in the area then she'd still live at home, which is why barely anyone recognised her. She never spent the time socialising in Halls or at student house parties like we all did in our first years.

I called Nick but he didn't answer. Not surprising.

I called Dean.

"Hey, what's up?" he answered, sounding stoned out of his mind.

"I want to know if Skye ever took you anywhere for your rendezvous?"

"Matts, will you just drop it already?" He sounded tired and strained.

"It's important, please?"

"Fine, I'll text you the address of her place, but this is the last time I'm doing anything Skye related for you."

"Thanks, Dean, but you know that's not true."

He hung up with a frustrated sigh that told me I was right. Dean would do anything for me still, and he knew that I knew it.

My phone pinged a second later with an address. I swore under my breath. I knew where it was without pulling up my maps app.

I decided to go and pay her a visit. I hoped that there would be a chance to meet her adoptive parents and see a little more into her life, even if she wasn't as sinister as I was starting to believe.

With no-one around to stop me, Nick not answering his phone, and Dean high as a kite, I grabbed my coat and pulled on my shoes, pocketed my phone, and strode out of the door.

My phone pinged several times as I walked down the street. I no longer kept it on silent, a painful new habit I'd adopted since it ringing had saved my life. I thought about ignoring it but decided that it might be a smart idea to check in with someone about where I was going and what I was doing.

A missed call and a text from Dean, warning me not to go round to her house.

A text from Nick, telling me he got called into the station and couldn't answer the phone.

I ignored Dean and sent Nick a message back with the address I was walking to, with no context apart from that I wanted someone to know where I was going.

I admit that it wasn't a clever plan. Walking around alone, at night, to someone's house who may or may not be the person who pushed me into a river and caused the death of three of my peers. But sometimes you needed to grab the bull by the horns, and if my profile was right, then the killer wasn't necessarily a violent person. The poison, the manipulation, the sabotage, the anonymity – it didn't scream aggressor to me. More like calculated, scheming, and cunning. If I just showed up there, then there wasn't a chance she would have a murder plan in place. Especially if her parents were there. There was no safer place!

The house she lived in was on the other side of the village, closer to the lake than anywhere I'd lived, in a place we aptly called Waterhead. Her adoptive parents were minted, like she told me when we first met. It was a modern four bedroom, gazillion bathroom, detached house with a balcony, lake view, private drive, and garage, which was a massive plus. In Ambleside, parking was a ball-ache.

I opened the maps app on my phone to make sure that I was at the right house. I was. I had several more concerned messages from the men in my life, which I ignored.

Taking a deep breath, I walked up the gravelly drive to the front door. It was a stylish, glass-fronted porch in which regular people might keep shoes or umbrellas, but instead there was nothing but a post rack and a remote.

They must have had a doorbell camera because before I even knocked on the door, I could hear someone approaching from within. I waited patiently for the middle-aged man to unlock and open the door.

"We don't want to convert, thank you, and sorry for wasting your time." He made to close the door, but I put my hand out to stop it.

"I'm a friend of Skye's," I blurted, suddenly aware that I must have looked like a street urchin in comparison to his sleek athleisure.

He looked me up and down before baring his teeth in what I hoped was a smile. "Come on in, then. My daughter doesn't bring home many friends, I apologise for the misunderstanding."

"No worries, is she here?" I asked, following him through the porch and into the kitchen.

"She just popped out for a run but should be home soon, would you like a drink while you wait?"

"No, thank you, I just wanted to stop by and see if she wanted to study with me." I couldn't think of anything else in the moment and hoped that it would pass as an excuse for turning up to her house when she was out.

"Study buddies, a very sensible suggestion." He paused for an agonisingly long time before turning around again. "Is Skye doing alright at University?" Her name seemed foreign on his tongue, but he pushed onwards.

I tried not to notice and answered. "Yes, your daughter is really smart."

"I was worried that she'd been neglecting her studies, what with all the deaths on campus." He let the last part hang in the air, as if he needed me to elaborate.

"It's hard for everyone. I think they're taking it into

account with our grades, but I didn't think she knew any of them particularly well?"

"She knew them all, very well, she was devastated after the announcement of each. Poor girl."

"I... I'm so sorry, I didn't know that."

"How well do you know my daughter?"

"Well enough," I answered, unconsciously lifting my hand up to my neck brace.

"You're the girl they found in the river, aren't you?" he asked, his pale brown eyes sparking with intrigue.

I nodded, unable to utter another word. The man was intense. I couldn't tell whether it was just because of the wealth or something much more criminal.

"I'm glad you're okay, the others weren't so lucky."

"I wouldn't put it down to luck," I replied bitterly, thinking about how his daughter was my prime suspect in the deaths of my peers.

"Yes, of course. I'm sorry, that was insensitive of me." He drummed his fingers on the marble countertop as if he was itching to say something, or do something.

"I should go. I don't want to take up too much of your time, got to write those words!"

"Oh no, no, stay, she won't be too much longer," he begged, his eyes were empty, emotionless.

"I..."

He took a step closer to me, his eyes drinking in my appearance like I was a rare bird that he'd never see again. The hairs on my neck and arms stood on end as he approached. There was something setting off my internal alarms. Something apart from the general creepiness.

He smelled like petrichor, the smell of rain on a warm day. It reminded me of something. Some repressed memory struggling in the depths of my brain to come to the surface.

"Come, let me show you the rest of the house," he announced, the creepiness edging away and being replaced with a businessman-like conduct.

"Alright," I responded, trying not to let him see me reaching for my phone. I knew that something wasn't right, but I usually got that feeling far too late. I wanted to be ahead of the curve this time.

While Skye/Emma's dad walked in front of me, pointing to parts of the house or the decor and commentating on it like a tour guide at a museum, I was sliding my phone out and typing a message to Nick, annoyed at myself for not giving him more information earlier.

I snapped back into the present when my guide turned around suddenly, to make sure I was listening, no doubt. Luckily, I'd finished my secret task and was tuning back into crazy FM.

"You said earlier that Skye was devastated when her friends died? Does she talk to you about everything?"

"Oh yes, we are a very open family. She tells me everything, there isn't a part of her life that I don't know about. Why do you think she goes to University here and not some far away city?" He scoffed at the last part, as if it was stupidly obvious.

I was beginning to feel sorry for Skye, no wonder she was the way she was.

"Ah, you must know about her boyfriend, Dean, then?" I ventured, trying to keep my face expressionless.

"Oh, yes, she talks about Dean all the time. I haven't seen the boy in a while, though," he rambled, a faraway look on his face.

"Haven't seen him in a while?"

"Oh yes, he used to come over a lot in the beginning, now I think she goes over to his, embarrassed of us, I

162

reckon."

"Us? I haven't had the pleasure of meeting your wife yet, is she in?"

"I'm afraid my wife is quite ill, she's sleeping." He said it sweetly, but his eyes turned dark, and his body stiffened.

"I'm sorry to hear that, I hope she gets better soon, and hope I'm not disturbing her by being here."

"Nonsense, she won't hear you, let us continue," he baulked, regaining his tour guide persona.

"I really have to get going now actually, I'm sure I'll be back another day to see the rest of the house," I said apologetically, pulling my phone out of my pocket to pretend to check the time.

Just then, it started to buzz.

It was Nick.

I shook the phone apologetically and answered it, making sure not to turn my back on the man.

"Hey, Nicky, yeah, I'm coming soon," I started, cutting off whatever he was about to say so that he'd know I was worried.

"Okay, I'm outside now, can you come out?" Worry laced his words, and he was doing a bad job of hiding it.

"Yep, I'm coming out now, sorry I'm late," I tried not to look at Skye's dad's face as I acted out my scene.

I didn't hang up the phone, I just stuffed it into my pocket so Nick could hear what was happening. I wondered whether he really was outside, or whether that was just so I would feel better.

"Nicky?"

"Yeah, my boyfriend," I replied with a shy smile.

"Your boyfriend's a cop?"

"How do you know that?"

"I know more than you think." He grinned boyishly.

"What do you mean by that?" I asked, suddenly not

bothered about keeping my cover intact, wanting to end the games and get to the bottom of the weirdness.

"I know a lot about you, Matilda, you aren't a friend of my daughters at all. She loathes you after you tried to steal her boyfriend. Dean."

"Wait, what?"

"Don't act stupid with me now, Matty, you've almost worked it all out."

I felt like a ton of bricks had been dropped on my chest. The way he said my full first name and the name my friends called me interchangeably freaked me out. It wasn't Skye. She wasn't the criminal mastermind I thought she might have been. It was him.

"Who are you? And why are you doing this?"

"Sorry, I didn't introduce myself. I'm Edward Seaton, owner and CEO of Seaton Security." His chest puffed up proudly as he spoke. "And as for why I'm doing this, well, I just want to see my baby girl happy."

"So, killing her friends and terrorising her University is the way to do that, then?"

"You've got it all wrong, I rescued her, took her in as my own, I'm not a bad guy."

"You didn't kill them?"

"Admittedly, I was the catalyst in the deaths of those girls, but it was Dean who killed them."

"And how do you figure that one?"

"If he'd died instead of Sarah, if that stupid girl had done her job properly, then they would have lived."

"Dean?"

"Yes, Dean, who else!" he spat venomously.

"So, all this was about Dean? You didn't like him dating your daughter so you thought it would be easier to kill him off?"

"Not easier, better, for everyone involved. The boy's a

trainwreck, you know that."

"That is so messed up, who are you to decide who lives and who dies?"

"Oh, it's easier than you'd think." He smiled creepily, sending a shiver down my spine.

"And Tommy?"

He laughed maniacally. "That wasn't actually me. I guess your boyfriend wasn't observing the Highway Code and got himself into that fatal tangle all on his own."

My heart stopped. My ears rang. Edward didn't kill Tommy. I did. I forced myself to keep him talking despite the life-changing revelation.

"It was you that pushed me?"

"Indeed, and if that cop wasn't sniffing around you like you're in heat, then you would have perished, too. But no, you just won't go, will you?"

"And, just so I'm getting this right, you wanted to kill Dean, but you didn't care whether I got hurt either, because you think I stole your daughter's boyfriend?"

"Correct."

"So, hypothetically, if you confessed to all this and got caught by the police, then you wouldn't have to kill me?"

That's when he lunged at me, his hand going to my pocket where my phone was. I let him grab it.

He was almost foaming at the mouth when he saw Nick's name on the screen and the live call.

"P.C. Wilde, how lovely of you to be with us." He switched back to businessman mode, his voice chirpy and charming. "I suggest that you don't try anything, or they all die."

I couldn't hear what Nick was saying on the other end of the line, but I knew that they would have to get someone in to negotiate. Nick wouldn't be the best person for that.

Edward hung up the phone.

"Skye isn't really out on a run, is she?"

Edward laughed. I watched his movements carefully, knowing that he was going to try something. He was desperate now, like a cornered rat. And we all know what cornered rats do; they attack.

I looked around sneakily to see if there was anything I could use as a weapon, worried that if I didn't subdue him then Skye and her mother would be in danger. I thought it would be best to keep him talking. We all know how evil villains spill their plans when they think the hero has no chance of escape.

"What was the end game here, Edward? You should have known Nick wouldn't be far behind me."

"I thought the young officer had put some distance between the two of you, arguing about boys, the little slut that you are."

"You bugged the house?"

"Of course, how would I know exactly what you knew if I didn't?"

"How did you do it?"

"I have my ways, a bit of blackmail, a bit of coercion, sometimes it doesn't take much..."

"Caitlyn helped you?"

"She didn't have much choice, but when I learned that the two of you were at odds, living in the same house – I knew I had an opportunity."

"You're sly, I'll give you that. Tommy's phone, was that you? Who did you blackmail to steal that?"

"That was easy, our friendly local bar-rat Martin was delighted to have his drinks paid for for the rest of the year. I found out that he had a knack for pickpocketing at the bar."

"And what did you have on Dean?"

"Do you know why Dean doesn't drive?"

"No," I answered, wondering where he was going with that.

"A little uninsured hit and run when he was fifteen. The guy died, never caught the culprit."

"And you've been holding that over him, for what? So, he doesn't dump your daughter or blab about what a crackpot you are?"

It seemed like Edward was done talking. He dropped my phone on the ground and crushed it under his running trainer without dropping his gaze.

I charged at him, while his balance was off. He expected me to run, but not towards him. I caught him off guard and sent him tumbling across the wooden floor. He hit his head with a sickening crack.

I waited for a moment before crawling back over to him and checking his pulse. He was alive, but out cold.

I scrambled to my feet and ran for the front door, it was locked. I looked around for a key. I ran back to Edward's unconscious body and searched through his pockets.

My fingers closed around the cool metal of the key and I almost relaxed. That's when I heard the banging. Muffled screams from behind a thick door.

"Skye," I breathed.

What would happen to her if I left now? If I took the key and went out to Nick and the other police officers, would she be alright? Would her father wake and take his anger out on his imprisoned family?

I didn't feel like I had much choice. I knew the police would be able to help, but I wasn't sure they'd make it on time. I took off my coat and zipped Edward into it backwards, like a makeshift straight-jacket, lord knows he needed one, and sprinted to the door.

I rammed the key in the lock and turned, feeling the

tumbler's click made my heart soar with relief; I was nearly free.

Being the head of a security firm and all-round evil genius, Edward Seaton made sure that his house was secure. The key was a decoy.

Alarms blared and the shutters sprang into action. I looked through the glass fronted porch to see Nick and several other uniformed officers racing up the path towards the house. I watched them and the flashing lights of the cruisers disappear behind the shutters. I looked down at the key, seeing what I'd failed to see in my haste to escape; the biometric scanner.

"Who the hell is this guy?" I whispered as I spun around, determined to find another way out.

The frantic banging from upstairs continued. I was reluctant to go up there and trap myself, but I didn't see that I had any other choice. I just hoped that Skye knew how to sneak out of her father's crazy house.

On the way to the staircase, I checked on Edward to make sure he was still alive, - but not so much alive that he was going to come after me again.

He wasn't there.

Neither was my coat.

That was a good sign because it probably meant that he was still trapped, wrapped inside the makeshift straight-jacket.

I didn't hang around to wonder where he'd gone. He most likely knew that I'd set the alarm off and therefore knew my location. I sprinted to the stairs, grabbing a fancy-looking candelabra on my way through for lack of any other suitable defensive weapon choices. I hefted it in my right hand, ready to channel my legendary Primary School rounders swing.

The stairs were modern, made of clanging metal like a

fire escape, leaving no privacy and sneak-ability to the house. Edward would know where I was, for sure. I pressed on, happy with my candelabra and solid in my goal. Free the Seatons, avoid the killer.

I crashed up the stairs and followed the pounding noise of Skye trying to break the door down. In my head it sounded like a heartbeat, sinisterly loud and bass-y, vibrating through my very being.

I desperately wished I'd finished the tour now because I didn't know where I was going or what was around the corner. It could be Mr Security himself, for all I knew.

Brandishing the candelabra as menacingly as I could muster, I rounded the corner at the top of the stairs to find it blissfully empty, apart from the pounding at the door. I followed the noise, trying the step carefully on the wooden flooring so I could isolate the sound and make sure Edward wasn't around.

I reached Skye's door. I placed a hand on the dark wood.

"Skye?" I whispered through the door. My eyes darting around wildly, too scared to take my attention off the corridor.

"Matty! Is that you?" The muffled response came a moment later, as if she hardly believed it herself.

"It's me, how do I get you out of here?"

"The doors are on a system, biometric only assigned to him, you can override it by..."

I didn't wait to hear the response, a crashing noise from across the house stole my attention. I was so tight with fear now. Adrenaline was spiking my emotions. I just wanted to get out.

I slammed the candelabra down on the biometric pad over and over again until it sparked, crackled, and fizzled.

The door took its time to decide what it was going to do

and for a heart-stopping moment, I thought I'd screwed it. Then the lock clicked, and the door popped open a fraction.

"You were saying?" I bragged as Skye yanked the door open and looked me up and down.

Her hair was messy, and her makeup had run. She was wearing the same clothes I'd seen her wearing the last time I saw her, which must have been days ago. Her eyes were red and puffy, almost bruised with crying and a lack of sleep. I couldn't tell whether she was going to hit me or hug me.

It was the latter. She wrapped me tightly in her sleek arms, squeezing me gratefully. She let go suddenly as if she was embarrassed at her outburst of emotion.

"We have to go," she whispered, looking around skittishly.

"What about your mother?" I asked.

"I think it's too late for her," she answered, her eyes steely and bloodshot, with no more tears left to cry.

"If there's a chance?"

"Down the hall, door on the right, be careful, be quick."

"Where are you going?"

"We still need to override the system if we're going to get out of here!" she called over her shoulder as she skidded back towards the stairs.

"Crap!" I whispered, rocking back and forth on the balls of my feet, not knowing whether to follow or do as she asked. It would be better if we stuck together. We could overpower him if there were two of us, but we might be able to get out quicker if we split up. There was only one of him after all, he could only go after one of us. My internal monologue was going crazy, fuelled by adrenaline and fear.

I'd go find her mother. Although, according to Skye, it might be too late – whatever that meant, I couldn't be sure. Was she dead? Brainwashed? I had to find out for certain.

Following Skye's directions, I made it to what should be her mother's door, quickly and without interruption.

This door didn't have a biometric pad like Skye's or the front door, instead it was slightly ajar. That was never a good sign. I'd watched enough horror movies to know that whatever was behind that slightly ajar door wasn't normal, healthy, or in my best interests.

"Hello?" I called, pushing the door to avoid surprising anyone inside. "Mrs Seaton?"

There was no answer and no noise coming from inside the sinister room. I didn't want to go in, but what was I going to say to Skye? *Yeah, I didn't get your mother, the room was creepy as hell, so I bolted, hope you don't mind.* No. I was going to have to sack up and go in.

"Mrs Seaton?" I called again, louder this time, hoping that she would answer, that she was still alive.

I flicked the light switch on the wall to the right of the door, hoping that once the room was better lit it would be less creepy. It wasn't. Mrs Seaton was there, strapped to a bed with an IV line in her left arm. Her eyes were open, but they were vacant, like she hadn't seen or heard me.

So, Edward was drugging his wife and locking up his adopted daughter, murdering students, and spying on people through his security firm. What a guy. I crossed to Mrs Seaton's bedside. I took her hand in mine gently and called her name again. She lolled her head in my direction and smiled. It was not as encouraging as I would have liked.

"We have to go now, Mrs Seaton," I explained kindly as I began to unstrap and free her from her prison. She was once a beautiful woman, elegant. But now, she was sunken. She was fragile from lack of movement and her muscles had atrophied. Her skin was almost transparent and stretched across her bones loosely, showing the weight she'd lost. Her eyes were dull and sparkless, filled with a deep sadness.

She shook her head as I tried to pull her into a sitting position. Was she shaking her head because she didn't want to go with me? Or because she couldn't? I found out the answer: a prick in my neck and everything was black.

* * *

Despite Edward's passion for my demise, I awoke. The room was cold and quiet. Not a sound reached my ears. My eyes fluttered open, groggy from whatever sedative Edward had injected me with.

I blinked several times, trying to get used to the blinding light from the fluorescent bulbs overhead. I was laid haphazardly on the ground. I felt the damp soak through my clothes and deep into my bones.

He'd been in a hurry when he deposited me here, but not so much of a hurry that he forgot to bind my hands and feet. I wiggled into a sitting position, taking stock of my surroundings. The room was completely bare, with whitewashed stone walls and floors. A room that could only be the cellar; everywhere else in the house was modernised and sleek.

I wondered what had happened to Skye, whether she'd made it out, whether Nick was still trying to rescue me, whether Edward was still terrorising the village.

Waiting for Edward to come back was the only thing I could do. I couldn't get out of my handcuffs, and even if I could, I wouldn't be able to get through the door.

After Edward told me, with Nick listening, his dastardly plans, there was no way he could get away with what he'd done. No matter if I got out of here or not. This thought calmed me down. I'd done my part, I'd exposed the killer, whatever happened next didn't matter.

Yes, I didn't get the right culprit the first time around. And yes, I guess I was slightly off with the motive, but I was right about everything else. The means, and the fact that Dean was at the centre of it.

So, I waited.

And waited.

And waited.

Until, finally, I heard noises.

I opened my eyes, but I couldn't locate the source of the sound. I strained my ears and moved my head slowly around.

It was coming from the corner behind me. I spun around, thinking I'd see something there that I'd missed earlier. There wasn't anything. I heard the snap and crackle of static and the mystery was solved. It was a speaker.

"Glad to see you're awake, Matty, just in time for the grand finale. Sorry you couldn't be here to watch it in person, but as you like eavesdropping on conversations so much, I thought I'd let you listen in! Ciao!"

I scowled intensely, trying to figure out what he was plotting. Static buzzed again and I heard a voice that made me feel sick.

"Mr Seaton, if you let the girls go, we can work this out, it doesn't have to end like this."

"Oh, Dean, you greedy boy, you've lost them both now, and I'm afraid you won't get either of them back."

"Please, just come outside, they said they'll make you a deal if this ends now."

"This is going to end now, Dean, this is all going to end now."

"Matty! Skye!" Dean screamed, his voice hoarse and thick like he'd been shouting all night.

"Dean, come away from the house, we're going to try something else," said Nick comfortingly beside Dean.

"That's it, Nicky, take the poor boy away, he doesn't need to witness this, he couldn't take it."

"What is he on about, Nick?" Dean asked quietly, moving away from the receiver and towards Nick.

The voices were getting quieter, so I assumed they were walking away from where Edward had hidden the microphone.

"Ignore him, he's just trying to scare you," Nick assured.

A terrifying blast echoed through the microphone and a deafening whoosh of static burst the speaker behind me.

An explosion of some kind could only mean that Edward was trying to burn the house down – with all of us still inside? Some kind of murder-suicide thing? But why not just overdose us? He wanted us to suffer, that much was clear, but he also wanted Dean and everyone else to suffer too. Suffer with the hope that we could still be saved.

Then it came to me, Skye had been adopted by the Seatons' when she was nine, because her birth family died in a house fire. Could that have been caused by Edward, too? Or was that too much of a stretch?

I felt the heat despite the coolness of the cellar, the dampness soon turned humid and sticky. Whatever Edward had used to set the fire, he wasn't messing about. It was probably hastened by the use of some accelerant.

The room heated quickly. Flames burn upwards. Heat rises. I was luckier than Skye and her mother.

174

I quickly began sweating, from the stress and the heat equally. If I didn't get out, I was dead. It was that simple. I slid my wrists up and down, using my own sweat to lubricate the cord I'd been tied up with.

I was known for being claustrophobic. Everyone who went camping with me or participated in escape rooms with me will tell you this. I was panicking now. The feeling of being restricted in a burning house with a psychopathic killer was enough to make anyone feel claustrophobic. It was like an out of body experience. I was suddenly very aware of my skin, of my breathing. I willed myself to calm down. To not reach the point of unbridled terror, because I knew once I hit that there was no chance I could escape. My better judgement would go out of the window, and I'd break down.

My bindings loosened.

Sweat beaded on my forehead and dripped down my face, down my neck, down my arms and legs. I was slick with it.

I loosened the cord even further, waiting as long as I dared before trying to slide my hands free. It was hard work, and my hands were red raw by the time I got them free. I cried with relief, thick tears with soft sobs.

My feet were bound with the same cord. After getting my hands free, it was no time before I'd untied my feet.

I sprinted to the door, slamming into it with all my might, which would have been a smart idea if I knew it was locked. Not so much when I realised it had been unlocked the whole time... I crashed to the ground, ungracefully.

There wasn't time to waste. I could feel the heat pouring down the cellar steps like I'd reached the summit of an active volcano.

I took the steps two at a time, feeling the smoke thicken with each one. I pulled the collar of my shirt up over my

175

nose and mouth to filter out some of the filth.

Edward didn't show me the cellar during his tour, which I was really regretting not finishing. I resorted to feeling around in the low visibility of the smoke, looking for an exit.

Except the only exit I knew of was locked down.

Time to find the back door.

I heard the smashing of glass coming from somewhere in the distance. I hoped it was just damage from the fire, and not some intense battle between father and daughter that I was missing.

I walked in what I remembered was the opposite direction to the front door, hoping to at least reach the kitchen where I hoped the door to the adjoining garage was.

Skye seemed to have the same idea. I saw her crawling underneath the bulk of the thick grey smoke towards the kitchen. I got down lower and followed her, unsure that if I shouted she'd be able to hear me. Or, that Edward would hear me.

I waited until I was directly besides her.

"Skye! You're okay?"

She looked shocked and relieved. "You got out!"

"We need to find an exit, what's the garage like?"

"Our best chance," she spluttered, the smoke reaching her lungs.

We crawled towards the garage door, Skye reached up and tried the handle. It was our lucky day. It was unlocked.

She pushed it open, still squatting close to the ground.

I pulled the door closed behind me. The garage had fared better than the rest of the house and wasn't as filled with smoke. We gulped in several breaths of fresh air before doing anything else.

I looked back at the door, hoping that Edward wasn't close behind us enough to see where we'd gone. I looked at the door handle to see if there was a deadbolt. Not that lucky.

I gazed around to see what I could use to blockade the door. The garage was immaculate. Bikes had their own mounts, boxes were neatly stacked, and tools were systematically stored in caddies.

Not for much longer, I thought mischievously.

"Skye," I said as loud as I dared, voice husky from the smoke inhalation. "I'm going to blockade the door. You figure a way to get us out of here."

"On it!" she replied, with a sarcastic salute. She skirted around the side of a large SUV and out of sight.

I grabbed tool caddies and boxes, dragged them over to the door, and began arranging them haphazardly to create a chaotic blockade wall.

Once I was happy with my work, I listened beside my creation for any signs of movement in the house beyond. It seemed like Edward hadn't realised where we'd gone. That, or he had passed out from asphyxiation. Hopefully the latter.

"Skye," I probed, "how's it going?"

I rounded the SUV and saw her fingering several remote controls – all different shapes and varying in number of buttons.

"One of these has to be the garage door, right?" She sounded frustrated and on the brink of panic, as if it had just dawned on her that we might not be able to escape.

"You'd think," I replied.

I watched for a moment, staring at the assembled buttons. They all looked out-dated in comparison to the rest of the tech I'd seen in the house. I left her to it, not wanting to stress her out more by trying to help.

I looked around. Smoke was now seeping out from the gaps in the blockade. We didn't have much time. If Edward was really hell bent on destroying the house, then he would make his way to the kitchen and cause a gas explosion with the oven. I shuddered at the thought, the thought that I was trying to anticipate our psychopathic captor's next move.

The door to the garage was metal and didn't look as strong as the shutters Edward had installed around the rest of the house. I wondered if he had some kind of tool that could break through it.

Returning to the immaculate tool caddies, I began sifting through drawers, not sure of what I was looking for.

"What are you doing, Matty?" Skye shouted from across the double garage.

"Looking for a tool to get the door open!" I shouted back, not caring whether Edward would hear our voices, as the smoke was becoming thicker by the second.

Amongst the possibilities were screwdrivers, a small hatchet, and a hammer. Not ideal, but probable if there was a way to jimmy it open. I crossed to the large sliding door with my haul. Skye was no longer trying to find the magic button but watching me carefully as I hacked at the control box and fixings to no avail.

"Matty," she began. "The SUV."

"Brilliant, but if you don't have a key for the garage door then how are you going to find the key for that."

"Key-pad." She grinned from beside the driver's door.

"Bloody millionaires," I cursed as I bombed it round to the passenger side.

Skye unlocked the car and we jumped in, glad of the fresher air within.

"Seatbelt," Skye ordered. "It's going to be a bumpy ride."

I obliged, clicking the seatbelt in place shakily.

A deafening blast erupted from the house, blowing out the blockade and sending garage debris over the windshield of the SUV. Flames sputtered and raged through the gap and licked around the wheels hungrily. I barely had time to wonder if I was right and if Edward had caused a gas explosion in the kitchen.

"Now!" I screamed, as Skye shifted the car into reverse.

"I know!" she screamed back.

I held on for dear life as she put her foot down, eyes closed, and body rigidly tensed.

Half a second later we collided with the large, metal garage door, and for a heart-breaking moment we sat there, unmoving. The door was strong. Stronger than we'd anticipated. An explosion in front of us was something else we hadn't anticipated. The airbags – they blew up in our faces, stopping our battered bodies from splattering against the dashboard.

Skye was determined. She thrust the car into drive and pulled forward, the sound of grinding metal reverberated through my bones. She battered the door again.

Flames roared towards us as they tasted fresh oxygen from the outside.

We still weren't out.

The car was heating up uncomfortably fast now. Sweat streaked down Skye's soot-stained face, her eyes irritated and pink from the smoke and other fumes, but she looked as determined as ever. I couldn't help but admire her in that moment. Everything she'd been through with Edward, keeping his secrets for so long – if she knew about them in the first place, that is. To now bring it all crashing down around him, everything he'd built, everything he'd done for her.

"Third times the charm!" she squealed, as the tires

screeched and spun in protest.

We broke through the door at great speed and careened down the drive onto the street.

Skye didn't lift her foot. Her face was pale with shock. Paler than usual. A lamppost put a stop to Skye's joyride.

She laughed.

I looked at her. And I laughed, too.

I closed my eyes and said a silent thanks to the maker of the SUV.

"We did it," I cried, punching her arm triumphantly.

"We did it!" she repeated gleefully.

A knock came on the window and we both screamed. The windows were blackened from the fire, and we couldn't see out.

"Police!" a voice announced from the street.

We unbuckled our seatbelts and opened the doors.

I don't know if they expected to see Edward, but they looked surprised to see two soot-coated students.

The streetlight was bright overhead, and it was almost impossible to make out faces and voices in the cacophony of emergency service vehicles.

A figure came crashing through the line of police and barrelled towards me. I was startled, still on high alert when he embraced me tightly, squeezing the fresh air out of my battered lungs. I relaxed into him, not knowing who he was, but just glad that he wasn't trying to kill me.

He pulled back enough for me to see his uniform.

"Nick?" I asked stupidly.

"You are a prize idiot, Matilda Darcy," he responded. No hint of annoyance accompanied the words.

"Why, thank you, officer," I laughed.

He dropped my battered, blackened body and held me at arm's length to survey the damage.

"Ooh." He sucked in air, grimacing.

"Rude."

"Let's get you looked at." He grabbed me by the arm and led me to one of the ambulances on standby.

That was the first chance I got to see the house, the damage that Edward had done to his family home. It was crumbling, blazing destructively despite the efforts of the fire service who were dousing it with their hoses.

Behind me, Skye was being interrogated by P.S. McNally, who was wrestling the weeping girl into handcuffs and reciting to her the Right to Silence.

"Stop!" I screamed, pulling out of Nick's grip.

"What is it?" he complained, following me as I slipped away from him.

"Skye had nothing to do with it, it was all her father, Edward!"

"But, how?" he asked, confused.

"You have to let her go!"

"If she's innocent, she will be let go, later."

"Screw the system!" I screamed, stamping my foot like a petulant child.

"Matty, I know you're upset, you've been through a lot, but you need to calm down."

"But-"

"No buts, that's not how this works," another officer said from beside Nick, grabbing my arm and stopping me in my tracks.

"Matty, just be glad it's not you in cuffs," Nick said grimly.

"Why would it be me?"

"The surveillance system was activated, sending an officer to the house, something that happens during a B and E."

"I didn't break in, that's not what happened."

"That's what they'll interview you about to find out."

I collapsed against him, exhausted from the events of the evening and not in the mood to spend the night in the cells at the police station.

Nick led me to the ambulance, unresisting.

Behind the police cordon, Dean shouted my name, waving his arms like a maniac. I waved him off half-heartedly, not having the patience to listen to his complaining.

PART SIX

EDWARD

The aftermath of the fire was devastating. Fortunately, it was a detached house, otherwise it would have spread like wildfire through the surrounding residential areas.

We lingered on the side of the street for what felt like hours while the firefighters battled the blaze – pumping water straight from the lake – waiting for the paramedics to clear Skye and myself, and for the police to take initial statements.

Dean had apparently called my friends because the five of them were waiting for me once I was discharged. Nick begrudgingly stayed on the scene.

"Matty, oh my god," Dee whispered, grabbing me tightly and pulling me into what turned into a group hug.

"I'm okay," I reassured them, escaping from the friendliest mosh pit.

"You scared the crap out of us," Lily jabbered.

"When did you all get back?" I asked stupidly, wondering how they'd all materialised so quickly from their separate plans.

"Dean called us and told us you were about to do something stupid, so we came to help," Hugh answered, a strange expression on his face. Was it guilt? Embarrassment?

"Ah," I said, looking at Dean reproachfully. "My white knight."

"I'm so sorry, Matty, I should have been there with you," Dean blubbered, hanging his head.

"We had it handled."

"Clearly," Danny chirped in. "Beautifully done."

I couldn't help but smile. Danny was usually so serious and sensitive, but he had his moments of comic relief. I was grateful for it.

"Let's go home," Hugh suggested, draping his jacket over my shoulders, not caring that I'd return it smelling of smoke and grime.

We began walking, huddled together, talking about what happened. I told them everything and they listened carefully without interruption until the end.

"Why didn't you find the control box for the security system?" Danny asked, his step matching mine casually.

"I... what?"

"A security system that advanced would need a whole rig, and a failsafe, too. If you disabled it then you could have walked out the front door."

"Alright, smarty pants, where would you keep a control box?"

"The garage," Danny grinned.

"Naff off!" I exclaimed in disbelief.

"I'm serious," he laughed. "Or a server room, if he had other things on the go."

"Great, next time I get kidnapped by a serial killer, you're coming with me. Skye didn't know how to find your mysterious control centre."

"Deal," he said, bumping my hip with his as we walked.

"And what about Mrs Seaton?" Lily said in a small voice. "That was sickening."

We all nodded in agreement, nothing more could be said. We had a moment of silence, thinking about the torturous life Skye's adoptive mother must have had married to Edward.

No-one spoke again for a while.

"I'll leave you here," Dean announced once we'd reached the roundabout near the place I'd nearly died previously.

"Why? Come back with us," Hugh pressed.

"I shouldn't." Dean was acting strange.

"Come on, man, you're the reason we're all together tonight, come have a drink with us."

"I am the reason. I'm the reason Edward killed all those people. I'm the reason Matty nearly died, TWICE! I should stay out of your way; it'll be better for the lot of you."

"Dean, no, it isn't your fault, he was a psychopath!" Hugh grumbled, facing Dean with an intense stare.

Dean looked at me. Waiting for me to agree with one of them.

"Come back with us," I asked, seeing the looks on my friends' faces.

That was enough for him to give in.

I was speechless that he put so much blame on his shoulders. Yes, Edward did those things because of Dean, but if it wasn't Dean, it would have been some other boy. I forgot how sensitive Dean was. How he broke down when we found Nina, how he wasn't afraid to cry in front of me, how he wears his heart on his sleeve all the time.

The others made small talk and chatted about their days to keep the awkwardness from seeping in. They never really liked Dean, but I think after tonight they had more respect for him than ever.

Back at the house, our other housemates were milling around in the kitchen, Caitlyn amongst them. She nearly fainted when she saw the state I was in.

"What the bloody hell happened to you?" Rhys asked, somewhat insensitively.

"Someone else explain, I'm going to grab a shower," I responded, deflated and exhausted.

I squeezed Dee's arm before opening my bedroom door.

I closed the door behind me and leant against it, the weight of the evening crashing down on me.

I cried as I grabbed my towel and shower caddy, the tears streaking down my soot-blackened face.

A soft knock came at my door as I was about to open it. It swung open slowly a moment later.

"Caitlyn?"

"Matty," she said, closing the door behind her and blocking my exit.

"I am so, so, so sorry," she began, tears streaming down her pale, freckled face.

"No," I stopped her. "You don't get to be sorry, you helped him!"

"I didn't know what he was going to do!" she protested.

"What did he have on you?"

"It wasn't like that..."

"Enlighten me, what was it like?"

She flushed bright red, searching for the right words to make her seem like she was justified.

"He didn't blackmail you," I realised. "What did he offer you? How much was I worth?"

"He– it doesn't matter," she flustered.

"It matters to me!"

The door opened again, forcing Caitlyn further into the room. Our housemates gathered outside the open door.

"Go on, tell them," I commanded. "Tell them how you sold me out, how you worked with the serial killer who killed our friends, and for what?"

My friends looked like they were about to jump in at any moment and stop me from wringing her neck, but they paused at my words, looking at Caitlyn apprehensively.

"He put me in touch with a talent agent, but–" she admitted, her eyes wild and unblinking.

That's when they pulled her out of the room. I know that Hugh, Jamie, and Dee would have loved to see me pound her, but Rhys and Kris pushed themselves to the front of the mob and defused the situation, removing the betrayer from our midst.

I collapsed onto my desk chair, the anger bubbling away, the red mist clearing.

Hugh herded the rest of them to the kitchen while Lily hovered in the doorway.

"Let's get you cleaned up, ey?"

I nodded, letting her pick up my cast away shower stuff and walking me to the shower to avoid more social interaction, or perhaps to stop me from hunting her down.

I showered for ages, letting the warm water wash away the soot, smoke, and the emotional pain from my body, and imagined it all swirling down the drain.

To say I felt new and reborn would be a cliché, but I did feel a lot lighter. Maybe it was the lack of smoke smell that had been a constant reminder of Edward's insanity, but whatever it was, it worked.

I sat at my desk and wrote in my diary, not able to face my friends just yet. I wrote every detail of what happened, not so that I would never forget, but so that I could get it off my chest. Taking it out of my brain and immortalising it in ink instead. It was better that way.

Finally, I made my way out of my room, fresh and clean, to my friends gathered in the kitchen drinking and laughing together. It made my heart warm. I joined them, gratefully accepting a beer from Jamie, and taking a long, deep swig.

PART SEVEN

16th February 2020

Dear Diary,

Edward and his wife didn't survive.

There wasn't much I could do to get Skye released. I tried. Nick wasn't much help, either. The police had made him distance himself from me after the fire, worried that he was getting too close to the students involved, and not acting his station. Not that he did keep his distance, but he couldn't be doing things on my behalf at the station. My friends hovered around me constantly, making sure that I was doing okay under the circumstances. Dean was nowhere to be seen. He decided that he had caused me enough trouble and couldn't look at me the same since Edward made his confession.

"What happens now?" I asked, balling myself up tightly.

"There's nothing we can do," Nick replied, angling his body towards mine.

We sat on the settee in my student house. Just the two of us.

"What did the police say to you?"

"You know I can't tell you that," he said, a flirtatious smirk playing on his lips. I noticed that he hadn't shaved in a few days, a light spattering of stubble adorned his boyish face.

"You can tell me anything," I flirted back, shuffling that bit closer.

"Matty..." he whispered.

"Nick," I replied, looking at him expectantly.

"Ding-dong," Dee announced, her body framing the

doorway.

"Dee!" I blurted, snapping away from Nick and the magnetic field pulling me towards him.

"What are you two kids talking about?" she probed, hands on her hips. "It better not be *Crawler* related."

"What else would we have to talk about?" Nick said coldly, sliding his hand back, the one that I didn't even realise was creeping towards my leg.

"You *do* spend an awful lot of time here, considering the serial killer is dead and you're, you know, a respected member of society."

"That's true," I agreed, shooting Nick a look.

"I'll go," Nick offered, rising from his seat.

"I'm kidding, Detective Nicky," Dee laughed. "You know you're welcome anytime."

She crossed the short space and flopped herself down next to me.

"Seriously though, what are we talking about, because if I hear Hugh say another thing about Pokémon, I'm going to burst into flames."

"We were, um," I faltered, looking at Nick for help.

"Skye," Nick said.

"Ah," Dee said in a small voice. My friends still hadn't come around to the idea that Skye was actually helpful and innocent.

"I want to help her but there isn't anything we can do," I added.

"Well, I have some good news, at least," Dee said.

"Go on," I prompted, leaning forwards eagerly.

"Caitlyn moved out," she said with a triumphant look on her face.

"What?" I asked.

"When?" Nick blurted.

"She finished moving her stuff out this afternoon," Dee

explained.

We sat in silence for a moment, stewing on the new information.

"Does that mean she won't be arrested for her part in Edward's plot?" I asked, looking from Dee to Nick.

"I don't know what this means," he answered.

"Whatever it means for the case, we have a spare room," Dee hinted, "so, Skye can move in!"

I was taken back by her answer. I didn't think that Dee or the others cared that much about Skye, but it did make sense. She no longer had anywhere to live, no family, no friends. We were all she had. She should absolutely come live with us.

"That's a really good idea," I said, finally.

"Yeah," Nick agreed, his eyes glazed over in thought.

"When she gets out, that is," Dee continued.

She rambled on for a few minutes longer before prodding me back to attention.

"Yeah," I said, snapping back to the present.

"I was just asking you about the ceremony," Dee repeated.

"Oh, that," I said. I had managed to avoid thinking about the ceremony all day, the one that the village decided we needed to honour the police and civilians involved in catching the latest serial killer to plague the UK. Both Nick and I were getting commendations, rewarding us for our bravery in pursuing the truth and justice for the victims of *The Campus Crawler*.

* * *

Skye moved in several days after the ceremony, when she'd been released and cleared of all charges. We helped her move what little she had left after the fire into her small second-floor bedroom in our decrepit student home.

"We can take you shopping, if you'd like?" Lily asked, hefting a depressingly empty cardboard box out of my car.

"That would be great," Skye replied. "I don't have any money at the moment, the police froze all Edward's assets."

"We got you," Dee said, squeezing Skye's shoulder on her way past.

"Yeah, anything you need," I added, slamming the boot closed on my dingey 2005 Fiesta.

"Thank you," Skye sobbed, dropping the box of clothes she was toting, throwing her hands up to her face to catch the tears.

We converged on her, patting and squeezing whatever parts of our friend were nearest.

"It's okay," I cooed, pulling her towards me.

We let Skye cry, steering her up the stairs to her new room. It was healthy for her to get the emotions out, and, after everything she'd been through, it was no surprise that she was feeling so teary.

* * *

The rest of the semester was painfully quiet.

Nick stuck around, becoming a piece of furniture in our house on his days off. It felt like he'd always been a part of the gang. He played games with the guys and hung around with the girls and me for our ladies' nights. He said it was to keep his ear to the ground on campus, but I saw the way he looked at me when he thought no-one was looking. Maybe they were right, maybe I did have a thing for Detective Nicky.

We all went through the motions, going to lectures and handing in assignments. Mundane things.

"I can't wait to graduate," I said one day. We were all flopped carelessly on the grass in the park, bottles of cider open beside us.

"Me too, girl," Dee replied, watching Hugh dive for the Frisbee Jamie had thrown.

"I know this is going to sound strange, possibly demented, but I can't wait to get back into it."

"Back into what?" Lily asked, flipping her sunglasses up to see me properly.

"Catching criminals."

"Yep, definitely deranged," Dee laughed.

"I know what you mean, it must have been thrilling," Lily agreed, "even if you were going after the wrong person."

"Hey!"

"Ha-ha! She got you there, Matty," Dee squealed.

"You're already writing your dissertation on the last serial killer you caught," Lily said jealously.

It was widely publicised that I was the youngest person to catch a serial killer in modern history. Everyone was waiting eagerly for what I was going to do next. I already had several offers from some of the larger Metropolitan Police stations.

"Yeah, we should get to the library," I realised.

"But we're drinking," Dee said, holding up her bottle of cider as proof.

"Yeah, Matty, take a day off," Lily agreed.

"Fine, I guess one day won't hurt," I resigned.

* * *

Skye said that we didn't have to go to her parents' funerals. She understood that her adopted father had terrorised and tried to murder me, twice, and that was enough to make anyone want to skip the event. I'd told her that I wanted to be there for her, if she needed me, because she had been there for me when I had needed her, and without her I might not have been alive long enough to be attending Edward's funeral. She caved.

Besides Skye, Jake, Lily, Dee, Hugh, Jamie, Danny, Nick, and I, the only other people attending were the press. They wanted to document and make the *Campus Crawler*'s final resting place public knowledge, no doubt to draw even more tourism to the area.

"I'm so glad you decided to bury your mother separate," Nick said quietly as we saw the news vans parked outside the cemetery.

Skye nodded, tears threatening her perfectly made-up eyes. Jake gripped her harder, his arm wrapped around her shoulders protectively.

He turned to Nick and nodded. "Bet you're glad you didn't wear your uniform for this."

Nick laughed as he brushed over the creases in his black suit self-consciously.

"Although your shiny new medal would have gone well with either outfit," Dee teased.

Nick blushed. He wasn't so used to getting attention and being treated as a part of our group. He also didn't like it when people mentioned the commendation he got for helping uncover the truth about Skye's adoptive father in front of her.

I squeezed his arm gently, giving him a look that no-one else saw. He eased up and smiled slightly. His shoulder bumping mine ever so softly.

"Let's do this," Skye said, drawing herself up to full height and wiping all expression off her face.

* * *

The funeral didn't last long. No-one had anything pleasant to say about Edward. The funeral officiant was instructed to only say the bare minimum.

We all watched as the casket containing the charred remains of the *Campus Crawler* was lowered into the ground, a sense of relief washing over us as we realised it was finally over.

* * *

Nick showed up at my Graduation.

I'd invited him, of course, but I hadn't expected him to actually come. My Mum was over the moon when she saw him walking down the aisle of the cathedral towards her and my father. Nick, in his smart police uniform, medal shining on his chest, his hair slicked back like the first time I met him.

My heart skipped a beat when his eyes met mine from across the great cathedral. I smiled calmly and lowered my gaze, blushing.

"You invited Nick?" Lily asked, being the first one of my friends to notice.

"He helped catch Edward, which helped with my grades, of course I invited him," I replied coolly.

"Sure, that's the only reason," Dee interjected in a low whisper.

I scowled at her and pretended to watch the ceremony of other graduates unfolding before us.

The past few weeks had been busy. With the semester over and the *Campus Crawler* caught, we had to begin focussing on our new lives, fielding job offers, and planning the next stages carefully. With this, our tenancies had ended, and everyone prepared for the dreaded move back home. Nick hadn't been around much for this, whether it was because of, as he said, business at work, or the fact that he couldn't bear to see us all leave.

I spent the rest of the ceremonies stealing glances at Nick and catching his eyes on me every time.

When it was all over and the graduates were filing out of the great cathedral, with beaming smiles and laughing proudly, I looked for his face in the crowd, allowing the stream of my fellows to pass by me.

"Looking for someone?" a voice said behind me.

I spun around, adrenaline coursing through me with fear, like in the days of the *Campus Crawler.* "Nick," I choked.

His eyes locked onto mine and he smiled that boyish smile.

All the graduates and their guests had hurriedly left. I realised, then, that we were alone. Alone. I'd fantasised about this moment since I first saw him striding into the cathedral, since his eyes had met mine for the first time in weeks.

"I..." he began.

I pushed him against the cool stone wall of the great cathedral, bathed in shadows, my hands resting on his hips. He inhaled sharply.

His eyes sharpened and I knew. I knew that I hadn't imagined the tension between us these past few months, that the sense of longing was mutual. He carefully removed my graduation cap and brushed the stray strands of hair from my face. With strong fingers, he worked his way down my jaw to my chin, tilting it upwards towards him. With a short pause to look deeply into my eyes, waiting for my nod of consent, he closed the gap between our lips.

20th July 2020

Dear Diary,

Skye didn't get any of the insurance money from the fire, because her father had started the blaze himself. She did inherit his business, and she donated money to the families of the students he'd murdered, and the emergency services for their involvement in tidying up his mess.

Our University got extra funding for our criminology programmes, and people flocked to see the ruins of the house where Edward fought his final battle.

My life changed completely. I graduated as a hero, the only survivor of the serial killer they'd dubbed *The Campus Crawler*. It wasn't something I was proud of in many ways, but it was the reason for the success in my field. Not every graduate could say they had first-hand experience catching a serial killer. Even if he was dead now.

* * *

I don't know what else to say in this diary about it. I'm happy it's over. I want to be able to live my life again. But I am thankful for many things: my diary, Nick, my friends, and keyless cars.

THE END.

About The Author

I am a young author from Sheffield. I moved to the Lake District to get my degree in Outdoor Adventure and Environment BSc (Hons) and have been here ever since. I love climbing, kayaking, and spending all my spare time in nature. I am a bookworm, always have been, always will be, and I take pride in growing my book knowledge (an asset to any pub quiz team). I like to think that I am a fun person to be around; at least, my cat seems to think so!

There are many aspects of my life that inspires me to write, sometimes it's the way the bats dip over the moonlit lake on an evening stroll, or it can be more serious, such as experiences that I've had that I can't stop thinking about. I have found that these experiences always wriggle into my writing unexpectedly.

My book *Silent is the Crown* was my debut novel and it's my first experience of sharing the crazy stuff that goes on inside my head with the world.

www.blossomspringpublishing.com